About the Author

Jim Stevenson was educated at Ealing County Grammar School and at TS Mercury, a private Naval Training School on the river Hamble. He served in the RN for ten years then spent the rest of his working life as an engineer in the avionics business. He has produced a number of booklets, mostly autobiographical, for the amusement of his family, but 'No Consolation' is his first published novel. He is a young ninety-two years of age and a dedicated family man. He lives in Gloucestershire with his wife of seventy-two years.

No Consolation

Jim Stevenson

No Consolation

Olympia Publishers
London

www.olympiapublishers.com
OLYMPIA PAPERBACK EDITION

Copyright © Jim Stevenson 2024

The right of Jim Stevenson to be identified as author of
this work has been asserted in accordance with sections 77 and 78 of
the Copyright, Designs and Patents Act 1988.

All Rights Reserved

No reproduction, copy or transmission of this publication
may be made without written permission.
No paragraph of this publication may be reproduced,
copied or transmitted save with the written permission of the publisher,
or in accordance with the provisions
of the Copyright Act 1956 (as amended).

Any person who commits any unauthorised act in relation to
this publication may be liable to criminal
prosecution and civil claims for damage.

A CIP catalogue record for this title is
available from the British Library.

ISBN: 978-1-80439-541-7

This is a work of fiction.
Names, characters, places and incidents originate from the writer's
imagination. Any resemblance to actual persons, living or dead, is
purely coincidental.

First Published in 2024

Olympia Publishers
Tallis House
2 Tallis Street
London
EC4Y 0AB

Printed in Great Britain

One

It was dusk and there was a slight chill in the air. An elderly couple, Richard and Mary Fleming, were walking home after an evening out at their Seniors' Club. He leant on a sturdy wooden walking stick, and she held onto his arm. They were discussing their performance at the quiz they had just left and chuckling that they had come second only because he couldn't remember the name of Henry VIII's first wife. "I knew it was Catherine of Aragon really."

"Then why did you say it was Ann of Cleves?"

"Ah well, that was just a momentary lapse of... um…"

"Sense?"

"Well, that wasn't the word I was thinking of, but perhaps you're right." He grinned.

She squeezed his arm then looked up and noticed three young men approaching them, spread across the footpath. Two wore wooly beanie hats and the third had an old baseball cap back to front and a ponytail of dirty hair hanging down his back. "Let's cross over, Richard, I don't like the look of these three."

As they stopped at the curb in readiness to cross the road, the three hurried up to them and one of them grabbed Mary's handbag, trying to pull it away. She held onto it and shouted at him; he pulled harder, then punched her in the face. She fell and her head hit the pavement. As she fell, one of the others punched at Richard's face, but his head was turning so the blow landed on the back of his head but with sufficient force to cause him to lose his balance. As he stumbled, he swung his heavy walking stick to his left in an attempt to steady himself. Then, as he fell, he swung his stick with all his strength in a vicious low arc which made contact with one of the thugs' shins. He screamed in pain and fell to the ground clutching his leg. The old man yelled for help.

***

Arthur Mason was cycling home from an evening Skittle match at the Red Lion when he turned the corner into Harpers Lane and saw the couple on the ground. He shouted and rode over to investigate. The three muggers tried to run off, but the one that Richard Fleming had hit with his stick was still rolling on the ground, holding his leg and whimpering in pain. Ponytail kicked the old man in the side then, between them, they helped their mate to his feet and staggered around the corner. The cyclist quickly dismounted, and after a quick glance at the old man, knelt beside the woman who hadn't moved. He pulled a mobile phone from his pocket and rang for an ambulance, stressing the urgency.

In the event, a police car arrived several minutes before the ambulance. The driver tried to help the old man to his feet, but he had dragged himself over to his wife and cradled her head in his arms. He was talking to her and calling her name but got no response from her; she was breathing but her head was bleeding, and she was deeply unconscious. While the driver was attending to the injured couple, his partner spoke to the cyclist who told him that he saw what appeared to be two figures helping a third hurrying away, but he was more concerned with the elderly couple to pay them much attention. He gave what description he could, but it was scant at best.

When the ambulance arrived, the paramedic asked the couple's name and address then examined Mary Fleming carefully. He gently lifted her head and wrapped a large, padded dressing around it. Then, together, he and his partner placed her on a stretcher and lifted her into the ambulance. His partner sat with her, connecting her to various pieces of equipment while the Paramedic turned his attention to Richard Fleming. Richard had a sore head, and his ribs were painful. He explained that they wanted to get Mary into the Hospital as soon as they could, but would radio for another Ambulance to take Richard in.

"I don't think that there is anything too serious with you, Sir," he said, "but I'd like to have you checked over for concussion and have an X-ray on those ribs."

"No," said Richard plaintively, "I want to go in with Mary."

"I'm sorry, Sir, I really am, but I'm afraid these COVID regulations don't permit anyone else in the ambulance, and I shall want to be doing some more tests on her on our way, which will help to speed up things when we get there."

"Where are you taking her, then?"

"We'll take her to Elmington General. It is possible that they would want to transfer her to the City Royal, but the General is very well equipped for this sort of injury." He climbed into the back of the ambulance, his colleague got behind the wheel, and within seconds they were on their way.

During the wait for the second ambulance, the driver of the police car chatted to Richard, asking if he could add anything to the description of the muggers that Arthur Mason, the cyclist, had been able to provide. "The one that tried to grab Mary's bag was a scrawny, scruffy looking bastard with what looked like a ponytail and a baseball cap. I didn't get a good look at the others; I was too busy falling down." He smiled ruefully.

After about ten minutes the second ambulance arrived. They checked Richard over and then took him, too, into the General.

Two

The three muggers had not got far. The one with the damaged leg was unable to walk without support from his mates and once round the corner and out of sight they reluctantly stopped, and the one with the limp was able to lean against a garden wall while he tried to get his breath back.

"You'll have to stay here," said Ponytail, "We can't hang around, we've got to get out of here."

"But you can't leave me 'ere, Zack, I fink that old sod broke me bleeding leg. I'm in feckin agony, mate."

"All right, I'll call an ambulance, then, so give us your phone." He felt in his mate's pockets and pulled out his phone. He gave the name of the road but a fictitious name for his friend, then put the phone in his own pocket. "Don't want the filth getting hold of this, do we? And just you keep your big mouth shut, Denty boy, right?"

"Course, wotcha fink I am?"

They left him propped him up against a garden wall and then Ponytail and the other ran off. 'Denty boy' was in agony from the leg and sweating profusely. Everything started to swim before his eyes, and then he gradually slid down the wall and blacked out from the pain.

The ambulance controller tried several times to contact the person who had rung in, but Ponytail had switched his phone off before he left. The controller was tempted to treat it as yet another hoax call, but when he replayed the recorded call, he could hear what sounded like whimpering in the background, so he dispatched the next available crew which was some distance away. It was nearly thirty minutes before they arrived at Briars Close, but they could not see anyone where he had been reported to be. They drove slowly past, then, because it was a cul-de-sac, turned at the end. Halfway back, their headlights picked out a form lying on the ground against a garden wall.

They had found the mugger, unconscious and pale. They quickly checked his vital signs and found his blood pressure alarmingly low with barely any pulse. They lifted him onto a stretcher and into the back of the ambulance. The driver switched on the blue lights and siren while his companion radioed into the hospital to have them prepare for an emergency.

**

At the hospital, Richard had been examined and X-rayed, and was waiting in a small ante room for news of his wife's condition. After what seemed to him like hours, a doctor appeared and sat down opposite him. "I'm sorry that we've kept you in suspense for so long, Richard, but we have some good news and some not-quite-so-good news. Firstly, the good news, you've no fractures to your face and no sign of concussion. You are a tough old boy and no mistake. Your ribs are quite badly bruised, but, again, no fractures. Now, as far as Mary is concerned, I'm afraid that she has not yet regained consciousness, and is likely to remain in a coma for at a least a few days... but there is no need for concern. I'm sure that she will recover and probably be as right as rain."

"Probably?" said Richard.

"Well obviously we can't be 100% sure, but at the moment all the signs are good."

"You wouldn't lie to me, would you?" said Richard

"Certainly not, Sir, and I assure you that we will be doing all we possibly can for her."

"Thank you, I appreciate that. Can I see her?"

"Of course, but only for a few minutes. She won't know you are there, though."

Three

The mugger with the damaged leg was examined in the A&E department. His trousers were cut away to reveal that his leg was black and swollen just below the knee, and badly distorted. An X-Ray revealed the tibia was extensively shattered with splinters of bone embedded in the soft tissue and muscles. Asked his name, he was too incoherent to answer, so was wheeled into the theatre prep-room and the duty orthopaedic team was summoned.

At about the same time, Detective Sergeant Dave Manners was preparing to go off shift. It had been an unusually quiet evening. He pushed his arm into his coat as he scanned through the couple of emails and reports that had just arrived when something caught his eye. An elderly couple had been mugged and assaulted in Harper's Lane in Kings Dalton which was a village some three or four miles north of Elmington. It had been a small rural village, but had expanded hugely over the last twenty years when a light engineering company, manufacturing car parts, moved there from Birmingham. They had brought a number of their employees with them and, in response to the need to house them, a large estate had been built on the southern edge of the village. This in turn increased as it soon became apparent that its proximity to the M5 Motorway made it an ideal choice for commuters working in Birmingham or Bristol. Thus, what had a decade or two previously been a delightful little community of less than two thousand, most of whom knew everyone and seldom ever locked their doors, had become a sprawling metropolis sadly lacking in its once strong community spirit.

Manners would freely admit that muggings were not usually top priority in CID, but his mother had been mugged a few months previously and he privately nursed a deep hatred for muggers in general, and those who picked on the elderly in particular. He sat back down and reread the report carefully; three figures had been spotted leaving the scene with two of them seemingly supporting the third. The report had been radioed in by the driver of the patrol car that had attended the incident, and he had gained the impression from the cyclist who had stopped to help that the one being supported by his mates had been rather badly hurt. He had been unable to give much of a description as he was more intent on helping the old couple. He put the report on top of his pending file then caught site of a report from the local hospital advising that a young man had been admitted, an hour or so after the elderly couple, with a serious leg injury. Nothing really to connect the two incidents except that he had been picked up by the ambulance crew in Briars Close, which Manners knew was a turning off Harper's Lane, and Sergeant Manners did not believe in co-incidences.

He took his coat off and sat back down. He rang the hospital and was put through to the sister on the trauma and orthopaedics ward who confirmed that a male, thought to be in his late teens or early twenties had been admitted via the A&E Department earlier and was currently undergoing emergency surgery.

"*Thought* to be in his late teens or early twenties?" he asked. "Don't you know his age?" The sister assumed he had either been unconscious or in too much pain to give his details.

Sergeant Manners could not speak to anyone else as there was no-one who would be able to add anything further until the operation had been completed, and that was likely to take several hours. He should call back in the morning.

Four

The following morning, as soon as he got into his office, Manners called the hospital. He was pleased to hear that Richard Fleming had been examined again that morning and had been allowed to go home, although his wife, Mary, was still in a coma and there was no change in her condition. He was put through to the trauma and orthopaedic ward, and asked to speak to the sister in charge. "Good morning, Sergeant. I'm Sister Grant, but I can't add much more to what you were told last night. The patient was in theatre for over six hours and has only just been brought into the ward from the recovery room. He is heavily sedated and will not be in any condition to be interviewed for some hours. We are no wiser as to his identity; he had no wallet or any form of identification, just a fiver, a few coins and a bunch of keys. There was also a small screw of silver foil containing some greyish white powder; I've my own ideas as to what that is, but it has not been formally analysed, so I can't say."

Manners hung up and walked over to a door marked 'Detective Chief Inspector R Parker'. He knocked on the glass and poked his head round the door. "Got a minute, Guv?"

Parker listened without interrupting as Manners gave him a full heads-up on the situation then, when Manners finished and sat back, he nodded. "So what do you want to do, Dave?"

"Personally, Guv, I'd like to screw the bugger's scrawny neck, but I really must follow this up. We need to know who he is and who his mates were last night and how he came to get so much damage to that leg. I need to talk to the cyclist and to the old chap."

"OK, get on with it, then, and if you need any help, let me know. And keep me up to date, yes?"

"I'd like to take Pete with me if you've no objection?"

Peter Lee was a DC with many years' experience and was a good friend of Dave Manners. They played Rugby together for the Police County Fifteen; Lee was about six or seven inches taller than Manners and nearly three stone heavier. With his shaven head he looked formidable and physically he was, but he was also very astute with a quick brain and a phenomenal memory.

Manners returned to his desk, checked the addresses of Arthur Mason, the cyclist and the Flemings, then tapped Lee on the shoulder. "Come on, Pete, you're with me and you're driving."

They knocked on Arthur Mason's door, showed their warrant cards and were invited in. He asked how the old lady was and expressed his sorrow. They went over the statement he made to the patrol car driver and asked if he could remember anything else. Did he see anything that might account for the one mugger's limp? "Well, I can't be a hundred percent sure, but I've a feeling that as he was falling, the old chap swung his walking stick round and I suppose that could have hit the mugger's leg. Actually, I rather hope it did."

"How did you happen to be passing at that time?"

"I was on my way home from a skittles match. I play regularly for the Red Lion 'A' Team on Tuesday evenings, and if it's a home game, I use my bike so that I can enjoy a pint or two. For away matches, my friend, Bill Wilson, and I take it in turns to drive so it's only one game in four that I'm on the orange juice. I wish I had got there a little earlier, though, I might have been able to prevent the attack."

"Well, your intervention was certainly fortunate for the Flemings, and I'm sure that Richard would like the chance to thank you. We don't normally do this, but would you mind if we passed your name and address to him so that he can contact you if he wishes?"

"Not at all. I would like the chance to call on him to check how his wife is."

"Well, I'm afraid we can't give you his address, but I've no doubt that he will be in touch with you."

They completed his statement which he signed, then they thanked him and left.

***

Manners and Lee then went to see Richard Fleming. They rang his doorbell, and after a few minutes, Fleming opened the door on a chain and asked who they were. "Detective Sergeant Manners and DC Lee, County CID, Sir, may we come in and have a word?" They held up their Warrant cards and the old chap peered at them, then said, "Just a minute." They heard a phone being lifted, then three bips as he rang 999. "Police, please." A pause, and then, "I've two men claiming to be policemen at my front door, and I would like someone to confirm their credentials please. Yes, they said County CID. Thank you." He was obviously connected to County Police headquarters and repeated his request. "Yes, they are still here. Yes, of course, the one claiming to be Sergeant Manners is about five-ten with gingerish hair and has a slight local accent. The other one is a big, baldheaded, ugly bugger about the size of a small bungalow."

Manners choked back a laugh as Fleming said thank you, closed the door, removed the chain and re-opened it. "Please come in. I'm sorry about that but I've been mugged once this week and I've no intention of letting anyone into my house before I'm sure who they are."

"Quite understandable, Sir, but we did show you our warrant cards."

"You showed me something that you said were warrant cards, but I've never seen one before so they could be labels off a marmalade jar for all I know."

"Good point, Sir, and quite within your rights too. Although I rather fancy that my colleague here thought your description of him perhaps a little harsh?"

"Then I'm sorry. There was no offence intended. Although your colleagues at County Headquarters did seem to recognize it, didn't they?" he grinned.

Lee grunted and said, "Yes, and there might be a few sore heads at HQ if that description gets circulated very far." Then he grinned and said, "Fair comment, though, Sir, and no offence taken. I've been called worse things than that in my time."

"Then please have a seat and tell why you are here."

Manners explained that they needed to take a statement from him regarding the attack and asked if he could identify any of the attackers and if he had struck one of them with his stick. "I can't be sure, but I certainly hope so."

"Well, Sir, a young man was admitted to A&E a couple of hours after you and your wife were, and he had what I'm told is a very severe wound to his leg, just below the knee. So, if you had hit one it is possible that he could be one of your attackers."

"Very severe? Now you are just trying to cheer me up," said Richard.

"Well, he could prefer charges against you for assault," said Lee.

"Ye Gods! You are joking, I hope? Three young thugs try to mug a seventy-eight-year-old, disabled man and his wife and in doing so gets a clout on the leg? I would be more likely to get a commendation rather than conviction, don't you think? And by heaven, I hope your 'very severe' isn't an exaggeration."

His description of the three matched that from the cyclist but he could add very little else. He signed his statement and Manners and Lee wished him well and left.

As they walked back to the car, Manners asked, "Well, what did you make of him, Pete?"

"Actually, I liked him. It takes something to keep a sense of humour in his situation."

"In spite of you being a big, bald-headed, ugly bugger?"

"And that's quite enough of that, thank you, *Sergeant*."

"OK, I suggest we grab a bite to eat then head for the hospital and see if matey is in a fit state to answer some questions."

Five

Earlier that morning, around ten a.m., the patient showed signs of coming round and was heard whimpering. A nurse carrying a clip board went into the room, drew back the curtains and introduced herself. "Good morning, my name is Anna, and I'm one of the team that will be looking after you while you are with us. First though, I need to take down a few of your details. Can you give me your full name, please?" She held a pen over the clip board and looked at him expectantly.

"I want something for this feckin pain, I'm in bleedin' agony."

"Yes, we'll get you something in a minute, but first I need these details so that we can register you and log you in."

"I ain't telling you nuffin'."

"Now, come on, Sir, this won't take long, and then we can get you something for the pain and make you a bit more comfortable."

"Piss off."

The nurse left and found the sister. They both returned and the sister said, "Now look, young man, I know that you might be in a little discomfort, but we need to register your admission, so stop being awkward and give the nurse the details she needs."

"I want sumfin' for this feckin' pain."

The sister glanced through the glass panel of the door and saw Dr. Johnson, the duty doctor, just entering the ward. She attracted his attention and told him that they seemed to be having a communications problem. Dr. Johnson entered the room and looked at the man in the bed who was squirming and whimpering.

"Now, what's all this nonsense about not telling the nurse your name and address, etc.?"

"Piss off."

"Watch your mouth; I will not tolerate that sort of language in front of ladies. Now, we need your name, address, date of birth, next of kin and religion. That's not too difficult, surely?"

"No comment."

"No comment? What do you mean 'no comment'? I'm a doctor, not a policeman."

"I don't 'ave to tell you nuffin'."

Dr. Johnson paused, then nodded his head slowly. "You are quite right, you don't have to tell us your name, or your address or anything else we want to know."

The sister looked sideways at him with a slight frown while the patient smirked.

"Unless, of course, you want to stay here and let us treat your wound, to try and heal it and keep your pain at a bearable level. Oh, yes, and change those dressings. Dirty dressings are a sure-fire recipe for gangrene. You know what gangrene is, I suppose? No, of course you don't, and I won't strain your tiny mind with the gory details, but it's when the flesh goes rotten and then amputation is the only answer, always assuming of course that you can find someone who would be prepared to perform an amputation on an unidentified body."

"Balls, you gotta treat me."

"Well, you might not be entitled to free treatment, you see, not everyone is, so we need to be sure of your entitlement, if any. Now, are you going to give us the details we require?"

Silence for a moment.

"Fine," said Dr. Johnson, "your choice, then. Sister, would you be good enough to arrange for the immediate discharge of this – person – please? No hospital transport, of course, or medication."

He turned to the door.

"Wait, wait, you can't do that!"

"Don't be silly, I just have."

"All right, all right, me name's 'Arry Denton."

"Will you take it from here then, Sister?"

The sister nodded to the nurse, and she left the room with Dr. Johnson. "Dr. Johnson!" she said in mock horror, "I'm shocked! Shocked, I tell you. That was totally unprofessional of you."

"Yes," grinned Johnson, "wasn't it just. But I promise not to do it again. At least not to 'Arry, there."

The nurse retrieved her clip board and said, "Right, then, your name, please."

"I just told 'im." He nodded towards the door.

"So now you can tell me."

"'Arry Denton."

"Address? And don't tell me any porkies, because if you do, we'll find out for sure, and you heard what Dr. Johnson just said."

He gave her his address and date of birth.

"Next of kin?"

"Wassat?"

"What's what?"

"What you just said, next of sumfin'."

"Next of kin."

"Yeah, that, what is it?"

The nurse rolled her eyes. "It means your closest relative."

"Wotcha wanna know that for?"

She took a deep breath and resisted the urge to follow Dr. Johnson's example. "So that we know who to contact if, er, things should take a turn for the worse. Or someone to bring you in some clean pyjamas. Are you married?"

He gave a snort. "No chance."

"No, I didn't think you would be."

"So, I s'pose that'd be me Mum then."

"And where does she live?"

"Same place as me, of course."

"Thank you, Harry, you don't mind if I call you Harry? That wasn't too difficult, was it?"

The nurse left to report her success to the sister.

"All right now, Nurse?"

"Oh yes, Sister – except when I asked him if he was diabetic, he said no, he was British!"

"He didn't!"

The nurse grinned. "No, he didn't, but I wouldn't have been surprised if he had."

"Anna! You are incorrigible."

"No, I'm not, Sister, I'm British like 'Arry!"

They giggle. "Well, I'm not too sure of that though, I thought you were some sort of Welsh alien."

Their banter was interrupted by the arrival of Manners and Lee.

The sister told them that they now had a name and address but suggested that they speak to one of the surgeons before talking to Denton. "Mr. Connaught is the consultant orthopaedic surgeon that performed the procedure last evening, but I believe he is off now. I think Mr. McGrath, his registrar, is on duty. If he is not actually in theatre, I'll see if I can get him for you."

She made a phone call, then said, "You are in luck. He'll be with us in a few minutes. Perhaps you would like to use my office? As long as you don't get delusions of grandeur, of course." She led them to her office and pointed out the drink dispenser on the way. "The coffee in that thing is reputed to be almost fit to drink, so help yourselves."

Pete Lee collected two coffees and they settled in the sister's office to wait. Lee tasted his coffee and pulled a face. "Hm, this NHS coffee is almost as bad as ours."

***

They had finished their coffee and were discussing whether another cup might be classed as 'suicidal tendencies' when a surprisingly young-looking man with dark, curly hair and several weeks of growth on his face appeared at the door.

They introduced themselves. "I'm Detective Sergeant Manners and my rather large colleague here is DC Lee. Despite his appearance, though, he is relatively harmless – on occasion. We are from County CID."

The newcomer grinned. "Hi, I'm Bob McGrath and I'm Mr. Connaught's representative here on earth. Or his registrar, if you're taking notes. I assume that you are the two gentleman interested in our mystery man?"

"A mystery no more," said Manners. "We now have a name and address for him, but we would like to hear from you. You were attending the Op, I believe?"

McGrath looked around the room, and, seeing only the two chairs that were already occupied, perched on the edge of the desk. "Oh, yes, I was there, mopping up the gore as is my wont. What is it that you want to know; I'll tell you anything I can, subject to the patient confidentiality nonsense, of course."

"Anything you can tell us about the wound would be most helpful," said Manners, warming to this young doctor who, he suspected, was nowhere near as young as he appeared to be.

"Well, for a start, he was very lucky that Mr. Connaught was here. He is probably the finest trauma surgeon in the country, if not in Europe, in spite of his awful taste in bow ties. Had it been anyone else on duty I suspect it would have been an amputation job. Actually, it might well still be; the tibia was pretty badly mashed and we can't be sure that Sir's magic has been totally successful for a quite a few days yet. His repair job was very impressive, but even so..." He shrugged.

"The ambulance crew were apparently given the impression that he had tripped and hit his leg on the curb," said Manners. "How does that sound to you?"

"Total bullshit, if you'll pardon the medical jargon," said McGrath. "There is absolutely no way that a wound like that could have been caused by a curbstone. For one thing, the skin was not broken and there was no grit or dirt embedded in the area, other than what might have come from his rather nauseous looking jeans, of course. No, whatever caused that wound was, what I believe you chaps would term, 'a blunt instrument', and it arrived at his leg with far more force than a simple trip could have produced."

He paused for a moment, then continued. "It was, or is, a rather complicated issue. You see, the fact that the skin wasn't broken hasn't really helped matters. OK, it stopped any dirt and possible infection getting into the wound, but equally it allowed the blood from the internal damage to build up into a very, very large haematoma and caused extensive bleeding across a large area. This young man now has two titanium splints screwed into his bone, and a good many stitches in the soft tissue where splinters of bone from the tibia had to be removed. Also, for good measure, a fairly large vein was crushed and that had to be repaired, too. In addition, it seems that he was left lying on a cold pavement for biggest part of an hour, and probably unconscious for most of that time, which did him no favours. So, all in all, not a simple broken leg."

Manners was silent for a while trying to digest what he had just heard. "This, um, blunt instrument. Any idea what it might have been?"

"I'm not a forensic pathologist," said McGrath, "but, if you don't quote me, I would say probably a smooth round object perhaps about um, say, fifty millimeters in diameter or a little less."

"Could a walking stick have done it, do you think?"

McGrath thought for a moment, then, "Possibly, I suppose, if it was stout one, perhaps like the old bog-standard NHS wooden ones that the physios used to cut to length, but it would have to have been swung with some force, and really it would have been a very lucky blow. Or unlucky, if you were on the receiving end of it."

"How long before you might discharge him, them?"

"Certainly not for a while yet. We will need another X-Ray in a couple of days, and it will depend on the result of that."

Manners stood and shook McGrath's hand warmly. "Thank you, Bob, you've been a great help. We may have to ask you to make a statement, but we can arrange to do that here."

"No problem," McGrath grinned, "but it might have to be a somewhat filleted version of what I've just told you now!"

"Of course, but now we must let you go while we try to have a chat with this poor young chap."

"Then you need to speak to the lovely Sister Grant, and

you'll find that she is nowhere near the terrible ogre some of the nurses would have you believe."

They returned to the ward and found Sister Grant. "Thank you, Sister, that was most helpful, may we speak to – er – *Mr.* Denton, now?"

"I don't see why not, Sergeant, but it will have to be short, we wouldn't want to over tire the poor man, would we?" she smiled.

"Oh, that would never do," grinned Manners as he followed her into the side room.

Denton tried to raise himself up in the bed, scowled at Manners and Lee and said, "Oo are you?"

"I'm Detective Sergeant Manners and this is DC Lee. We are from County CID, and we are going to ask you a few questions, then we will decide whether to arrest you or not."

"I ain't saying nuffin'."

Lee moved towards the bed and lifted the sheet over Denton's leg, "Can I've a little look at his poor leg, Sister?"

Denton tried to squirm up the bed. "Git orf, don't you touch me! Nurse, get this great brute away from me." He was sweating profusely.

Manners said, "Well why don't you just try to help us a little? We would like to know who your two pals were that helped you attack that elderly couple the other night. You do remember them, don't you?"

"I don't know what you mean, I dint attack no one. Ain't dun nuffin'."

"Oh dear," said Lee, "it seems he wants to do this the hard way, Sister. Isn't there something that you need to be doing at the other end of the ward?"

Before the sister could remonstrate with him, Denton started whimpering, "Don't you go, Nurse. You can't leave me 'ere wiv these two. I ain't dun nuffin an' I wants a sliciter."

Manners shook his head. "It's all right, Sister, we'll leave this for now." He looked hard at Denton. "But we will be back."

Six

Richard Fleming was just making himself a cup of coffee when the phone rang. It was the Ward Orderly from Leamington Ward at Elmington General who asked him if he would call in.

"Why? What is it? Is Mary alright?"

"I'm sorry, Sir, but I do not really know anything except that the sister told me to ring you and ask if you could come in for a chat. Please go straight up to Leamington Ward and ask for the sister."

"Can I come now?"

"I think that would be best, Sir."

He pushed his feet into his shoes, grabbed a coat from the rack in the hall and almost ran to his garage and set off for the hospital. He sat quietly fuming at a red light, drumming his fingers on the wheel impatiently, then drove as fast as he dared to the hospital, found a disabled parking spot and hurried up to the ward where he found the sister waiting for him just inside the door.

She led him into her office where the Doctor who had originally treated Mary was sitting. He shook hands with Richard and asked him to sit down.

"What is it, Doctor, tell me, tell me, she hasn't...?"

"I'm so sorry, Richard, but I have to tell you that Mary has taken a turn for the worse. During the night she developed a haemorrhage in the brain and I'm afraid that it is serious. She is currently on a ventilator but there's no chance of her recovering any reasonable brain function at all."

Richard stared at him disbelievingly. "But you can't mean that she..." His voice trailed off.

The sister moved her chair closer to him and took his hand in hers. He appeared not to notice, just continued to stare at the doctor as tears started to course down his cheeks.

"Believe me, Sir, we've done everything we possibly can, but sadly we're now in the position that we have to consider switching off her life support."

"But you can't do that. It's Mary, it's my darling Mary, it's..."

The doctor and sister did all they could to try and console him. The doctor pulled a small flask from his pocket and poured some brandy into a water glass and gave it to Richard, who sipped it in a daze. They took him into the side ward where his wife was lying in bed, surrounded by machines and attached to a variety of pipes and tubes. "You can spend a while with her, Richard."

"Will she know I'm here?"

"That is possible," said the sister. "They say that hearing is the last of the senses that go, but of course she won't respond to you."

The sister sat unobtrusively in the corner while Richard held Mary's hand and whispered to her. After some time, he stopped talking and his head dropped onto the bed with his body wracked with sobs. The sister helped him back to her office and after a while the doctor returned. "I really am truly sorry, Richard, but, although it may sound trite, she is at rest now and no longer suffering."

The sister said, "Do you have anyone with you, Richard, or any family that we should call? Anyone who can stay with you for a few days?"

He nodded. "My son."

"Can I contact him for you?"

He handed her his mobile phone and muttered, "Tony."

The sister rang his son and told Richard that he was on his way; he lived about an hour's drive away and would go straight to Richard's home.

"How'd you get here, Richard? Did you drive?"

He nodded absently.

"I don't think you should drive home. I will see if I can get someone to drive you, there are usually one or two social workers here and I'm sure they will help." She spoke on the phone for a few minutes then said, "Betty will be with us shortly; she is a lovely girl and she'll drive you home and stay with you until Tony arrives. Would you be happy if she gives Tony the details about the Bereavement Office and so on?"

"Of course. Tony will want to arrange things for me any way. He's a great help to us, always has been." His voice was choking.

When she arrived a few minutes later, Betty proved to be a middle-aged woman with an engaging smile and an Irish accent that endeared her to Richard straight away. "Come on, then, me darling, let's be on our way."

She took his arms and led him down to the car park, sat him in the passenger seat and gave him the seat belt. She got behind the wheel and pulled the seat forward as far as it would go.

"Right, me darlin', we are on our way. I have the address and I know where it is. I live only a few minutes from you." She continued chatting all through the journey, although Richard neither replied nor, indeed, heard what she said.

"Here we are, then. I'll leave your car on the drive."

She took his keys and opened the door and ushered him in. "You just sit yourself down, me darlin', and I will make you a cup of tea."

Richard sat in his chair with his head in his hands, totally oblivious of her and of her non-stop chatter as she bustled around in the kitchen, clattering about looking for some cups and saucers and making a pot of tea. He got to his feet as he heard a key in the front door; his son, Tony, came in and put his arms around his dad, and they stood there a while, hugging each other with tears streaming down their faces.

Betty came in from the kitchen with a mug of tea in her hand. "You must be Tony."

"I am, indeed, and who are you?"

"I'm Betty McCleod. I'm a social worker based at Elmington General and I drove your father home just now."

"Well, thank you, Betty, that was kind of you."

"And would you have a mug of tea, young Sir?"

"No, but I could murder a coffee, if you wouldn't mind. White, no sugar."

"Ah, that would be no trouble at all." She returned to the kitchen and Tony helped his dad into his chair and passed him his mug of tea. "What the hell happened, Dad? The sister from the hospital who rang me was very kind and sympathetic, but she didn't give me too much detail."

"It was horrible, Tony. We were walking home from the Club when these three yobs mugged us. One of them tried to grab your mum's handbag, but you know your mum, she hollered and tried to push the sod away, but he punched her in the face, and she fell and hit her head on the pavement. One hit me too, but as I fell, I swung my stick around and I think it hit one of them on the leg, but I was concentrating on your mum, so I can't be sure."

"Do you know who they were? Did you get a good look at any of them?"

"Not really, Tony. It was getting dark, and it all happened so quickly. Luckily a cyclist came by and when he shouted, they took off. After kicking me in the ribs, of course."

Tony was clenching and unclenching his fists and was swearing under his breath.

"It is possible that the one I hit is in hospital, but I don't know for sure. The detective that spoke to me after I got home said that a young man with a serious leg injury had been admitted to hospital, although he didn't say which one. He gave me the impression that he could be the one that I hit. If it was, then I hope he was the one that hit Mary. Oh, God, Tony, it was just awful, I couldn't get any response from her as she lay there and she hasn't been able to speak to me since." He gripped his son's arm so tightly that he winced. "What am I going to do?"

"I know what I would like to do," said Tony, "I would like five minutes alone with the bastard, I'd beat the living daylights out of him."

"What, in the middle of a hospital ward?"

"How can we find out who he is, Dad?"

"I don't know, son, and for sure the police won't tell us anything unless, and until, they can lock the bugger up, and frankly I don't hold out much hope for that to happen."

Betty brought a mug of coffee for Tony and asked if he would be making the arrangements for his mother. When he agreed that he would, she told him where the bereavement office at the hospital was and explained what he should do. She was most helpful, and Tony made notes about whom he should inform, etc. as she spoke. When Betty was satisfied that Richard was OK and that Tony appeared to have everything under control, she gave Richard a card with her direct line phone number on it and made him promise to call her if he needed any help, or even just somebody to talk to. She squeezed his arm. "I'll let meself out." She left to return to the hospital.

Richard sat with his head in his hands, his body wracked with sobs. Tony wanted his dad to go back and stay with him for a few days, but Richard declined. "No, Tony, I can't leave while Mary is here. You must go home to Sally and the twins. I want to stay by myself, at least for a few days."

Reluctantly, Tony agreed that he would go home the following morning.

Seven

Manners and Lee returned to the station, and on entering the CID room, Manners went into his small alcove while Lee made for his desk where he saw a large poster propped up on his computer. It was a mock-up of an Estate Agent's sign with a picture of a Bungalow and, in large letters, 'Small Bungalow for Sale. Only Bald-headed, Ugly Buggers need apply.'

"Oh, how jolly humorous," he said. "Now, which of you mini morons has a death wish?"

"Can't think whatever you mean, Peter."

"Well, someone has spelt 'bungalow' right so that cuts the number of suspects down. Now, who in here can actually write, I wonder."

The door to Chief Inspector Parker's office swung open and he appeared. "OK, cut the crap, children, gather round and listen up."

He waited a moment then said, "I have just had a phone call from the Hospital. Mary Fleming died a few minutes ago."

There was silence in the room and, banter forgotten, he had their total attention. "Now, I want to know who the other two were with Denton and I want to know soon. Who was checking on his known associates?"

Beryl Watson was a short, dark-haired and attractive Asian detective constable and was a recent addition to the team. She had a quick mind and had already earned a reputation as a brilliant and dedicated researcher. "That was me, Guv, I haven't had time to really get into it in depth, but I have identified five likely lads. Well four *likely* ones, as one of them is in Winson Green prison serving eighteen months for aggravated assault. He is Charles Harvey, known as 'Chips'. The other less likely one is Denton's brother, Frank. He is five years older than Harry and apparently has had nothing to do with him for some years. He is married and lives some distance away."

"OK," said Parker, "but keep him on the list. Who else?"

"Zack Peters. Tall, skinny, smothered in tattoos and has a long manky-looking ponytail. Or should that be pigtail? I don't have an address for him yet; I can't trace a Zack or a Zachary so that probably isn't his real name but there are four Peters on the electoral register so it shouldn't be too difficult to narrow it down."

Parker nodded and Beryl continued. "Amos Miller, very large, does a lot of weight training. Afro-Caribbean appearance. I have three possible addresses for him, but again the waters get muddied a bit because Amos may not be his real name. Then there is Colin Jacques, same sort of build as Miller but a local man. He too has tattoos all over his arms and legs. Has some previous; two counts of assault, three of breaking and entering and one of GBH for which he got nine months, at on open prison, would you believe? Usually wears shorts and I have a definite address for him."

"Well done, Beryl, that's good work. Keep at it with the addresses, though, I need them ASAP.

"Dave, I want you and Pete to get back to the hospital and have another go at Denton. And arrange for a uniform to be on duty outside his door 24/7. No one other than medical staff to go in under any circumstances."

"We're on it, Guv." He nodded to Lee and they both left.

Parker said, "I want all of you on standby. As soon as we have the addresses for the other four, including his brother, I will want a synchronized pick up. Three on each. If they refuse to come in voluntarily, they are to be arrested. And I want them in separate rooms when they get here, let them see each other, but absolutely no communication between them. Any questions? No? Then that's all for now. Dave?" But Dave Manners and Lee had already left and were well on their way to the hospital.

Dave was on the radio making arrangements for a uniformed constable to be made available for duty at the Hospital and for him to meet them at Bolton Ward as soon as.

"How do you want to play this, Dave? Good cop, bad cop?"

"No, bad cop, even worse cop!"

Lee grinned. "Oh, great, can I be the even worse cop then, please?"

"Naturally, mate, you were made for the role!"

Eight

When Manners and Lee got to Bolton Ward, they were glad to see that Sister Grant was again on Duty. "If you'd give me a couple of minutes, Sergeant, I'll come with you, but at the moment the phlebotomist is in there getting a blood sample from him."

"Dave, please, and that's fine. What's the latest on his condition? Any indication of when he might be fit to be discharged?"

"Not for another few days, I'm sure. He has had a post op X-ray and Mr. Connaught is satisfied so far, but wants to be certain that the titanium splints don't cause any unwanted reaction before he will let him go. And then of course it is up to the physiotherapists; they have the last word. They will want to see that he can get up and down some stairs and can mobilize a bit before they nod."

"Thank you," said Manners, "but I've some news for you that may not be too welcome. We're going to have to put a uniformed constable outside his door. He'll have orders to allow no one, other than your medical staff, of course, to enter, under any circumstances. And also to ensure that 'Arry boy does not attempt to discharge himself. He'll try not to get in your way, and I'm told that he is house-trained – well, as much as any of our uniformed colleagues can be, that is!"

"Is that really necessary, Dave?"

"For him to be house-trained? Well, we do like to..."

"No, you muffin, for him to be here, I mean."

He saw the grin in Lee's face and realized that it was unlikely that he'd heard the last of that sobriquet.

"I'm afraid so, Sister. We have no option in a case like this."

"In that case I shall try to find him a comfortable chair," she grinned.

"No need to go that far," chipped in Pete, "he's only a copper, not a detective or anything important like that!"

The sister looked up as the door to Denton's room opened and the phlebotomist came out pushing her small trolley. "Thanks, Sister, I'm all done here, now."

The three of them entered Denton's room, the sister closed the door and moved to a corner of the room by the window.

"Now then, *Mister* Denton, you do not have to say anything. But it may harm your defence if you do not mention when questioned something which you later rely on in court. Anything you do say may be given in evidence. Do you understand that?"

"Are you arresting me?"

"Not just at the moment, but you are now under caution. So, think very carefully when you answer my questions, and I do want some answers from you."

"I ain't dun nuffin'."

"Of course you have. You assaulted two old people last Tuesday evening and got a crack on your leg for your trouble. Surely you remember that?"

"It weren't me."

"We know it was you and we have witnesses who can, and will, identify you. And you were picked up by the ambulance not a million miles from where the assault took place – so grow up."

Lee cut in, "We are not talking about just another rather nasty mugging now, 'Arry, this is manslaughter, or if we are lucky, murder."

"Murder? I ain't murdered no one."

"Unfortunately, the old lady that you attacked has now died, so that is manslaughter, at the very least."

"I din do it. It weren't me."

Dave said, with an edge to his voice, "Then who was it? Which of your two moronic friends was it? Was it the same one who hit the old man and then kicked him in the ribs as he lay on the ground trying to protect his wife? I want their names."

Denton looked around, obviously scared. "I ain't saying nuffin'. I ain't no grass."

"Then you are more stupid than I thought you were. If you co-operate with us, it might help you at your trial – if you get a good lawyer and a sympathetic judge."

"Are you 'resting me then? 'Cos I wants a sliciter."

"I just told you, we are not arresting you at this moment, but we will be as soon as you are discharged from here. Then we will find a nice cosy cell for you at the station where you will be looked after by some nice friendly policemen. And you just need to hope that none of them have had their mother mugged by someone like you."

"Well, if you ain't 'resting me you can piss off, I ain't saying no more."

"Are you really sure that you don't want to tell us anything?" said Lee.

Denton turned his head away and stared at the wall.

Manners turned to the sister and said, "Thank you, Sister, I think we'll leave this for now."

***

They left the room, closing the door behind them, and saw a uniformed constable standing by the nurses' station. "Sergeant Manners?"

Manners nodded. "And you are?"

"P.C. Carter, Sarge. I was told to report to you here for some sort of guard or protection duty?"

Manners beckoned him over to the door of Denton's room. "Inside this room is a gentleman by the name of Harry Denton. He is not currently under arrest, but he will be as soon as he is fit enough to be discharged. He was involved, with two others, in a vicious mugging of an old couple and the woman has since died of her injuries. He is refusing to co-operate and will not name his accomplices. I want you outside this door at all times. No one other than the medical staff are to enter under any circumstances, and I do mean no one. If anyone does try to enter you will record their name and the time. And Denton does not leave this room; if the medics want to take him somewhere, for an X-ray or something, you will accompany him and you will not let him out of your sight. If he is stupid enough to try and discharge himself, you will arrest him on suspicion of manslaughter – he is already under formal caution – and phone me or D.C. Lee here. Got it?"

"Yes, Sarge."

"Good, when does your shift end?"

"Eight o'clock this evening."

"OK, I will arrange for someone to replace you before you are due to go off. So now go and have a pee while we are still here, then you do not leave this door. The sister has promised to find a chair for you, but just make sure you do not nod off."

"No danger of that, Sarge. I'll be on the ball. Am I allowed to go in and see him?"

"No. Ah, on second thoughts, yes. Just go in but don't say

anything, just make sure he sees you and knows you will be here."

Sister Grant said, "Before you settle in, Constable, I must tell you about the COVID restrictions here in the ward. As you know, the restrictions have been relaxed quite considerably in the last couple of weeks, but we do insist that face coverings be worn for anyone having any contact with the patients. So, if you've cause to go into his room for any reason, we would ask that you wear a mask. Otherwise, if you are just outside the door you would not need to, but the choice of course would be yours."

"Thank you, Sister, I will do that, of course, but it will be a relief not to have to wear one all the time."

Manners watched Carter as he took up his post then thanked the sister again. As they got to the door to leave, Lee made a show of opening it for Mannners and waved him through with an exaggerated sweep of his arm and a bow. "After you, Sergeant Muffin," he grinned.

Nine

Richard Fleming answered his doorbell to see a slim, grey-haired man whom he thought looked vaguely familiar. "Mr. Fleming, good afternoon, I'm Arthur Mason, I don't want to impose on you, but I had to call to see how you and your wife are doing after that dreadful business the other evening."

Richard looked at him more closely. "Oh, of course, you were our saviour! Do please come in." Mention of Mary caused him to catch his breath and tears ran from his eyes. He waved Arthur Mason to a chair then sat himself. He took a deep breath and said, with a quiver in his voice, "I'm afraid my darling Mary didn't recover."

"Oh my God, Sir. I had no idea. I'm so terribly sorry. I wouldn't have bothered you had I known."

"No, no, I am glad that you called. We, um, I, owe you an enormous debt of gratitude. If you had not intervened, I may well have suffered the same fate as Mary. Although, without her..." His voice trailed off into choking sobs.

"Those hateful swine! Why on earth do scum like that have to attack decent, elderly folk? They surely can't expect there to be a fortune in the handbag of a..." He paused. "I'm sorry, Richard, I should control myself, but I do get so angry when I think of this. Do you know who they were by any chance? Did you recognise any of them?"

"No, I'm afraid not Arthur. All I can recall is that the one who grabbed for Mary's handbag was tall and skinny with, I think, a sort of ponytail, and one of them was quite stocky and had one of those ridiculous woollen hats pulled down over his ears, but other than that..." He shuddered. "Everything seemed to have happened so quickly. The detective who came to see me said that I may well have struck one of them with my stick as I fell. Apparently, a young man was admitted to hospital, although he wouldn't say which one, with a 'serious' leg injury shortly after the attack, and he may have been one of the attackers, but he wouldn't say more than that."

They chatted for a while and Richard poured a couple of glasses of single malt and gave one to Arthur. "I hope you're not tee-total, my friend?"

"Heaven forbid," grinned Arthur, "I am no toper, for sure, but I do enjoy the odd glass or two on occasion and this," he raised the glass in salute, "looks like nectar. Thank you very much and your very good health."

Eventually Arthur got to his feet and said, "I really must be going, Richard, I have enjoyed our chat and if there is anything at all that I can do for you please do let me know." He wrote his phone number on a piece of paper. "I hope we can meet again soon."

"Oh yes, indeed," replied Richard, "but until the funeral is over, I can't seem to concentrate on anything. I'm not very good company at all, I'm afraid." They shook hands and Richard thanked him again for his compassion and his company. He closed the door behind him, then leant against it as tears again coursed down his cheeks.

Ten

Two days later, and a slim grey-haired man sat at his breakfast table, staring into space. After about an hour he nodded his head – he had a plan. He collected his laptop and drummed his fingers on the table, then went into the kitchen and made a mug of coffee. He found a pad of paper and sat back at his computer. He stared at the screen for a while; he'd heard someone say that there was a method of browsing the net without leaving a trail, but he could not remember how to do it. He was more than competent with a computer, having used one for his work and, since his retirement, for his twin hobbies of photography and philately, but had never before felt the need for secrecy. He googled various key words before he spotted 'incognito'. That would be it. He nodded with satisfaction then spent the next two hours searching online and making copious notes on his pad.

He then opened photoshop and designed two small cards, a copy of which he printed, then deleted the files that he had created. He cut both prints to the desired size and stuck then onto a piece of thin white card to stiffen them.

Although he had lived near Elmington, a small-ish town with a population of about ninety thousand, for many years, he had not realised the extent of the facilities that the town had to offer. Two fancy dress shops, for example, and three private investigators listed on the web. Two of those were obviously franchises from large national concerns so he immediately discounted them. The third was a possible, though, then he thumbed through his copy of yellow pages and found a fourth. Even better; Hampton and Gillis ran only the smallest block ad in yellow pages, so not big enough to warrant their own website. He noted their address which was in the 'lower end' of town and marked them as first choice for what he needed to be done.

Eventually he closed down his laptop and made a number of phone calls to some of the local shops that he had noted, being careful to prefix each call with -141 in order to withhold his number. He was pleasantly surprised that most of the items he wanted were readily available, so he wrote out a shopping list which he pocketed then put on a coat and hat and drove into town.

He would have to try Hampton and Gillis, the private investigators first; everything depended on them being able, and willing, to do want he needed. If they could not, or would not, he would need to rethink his entire idea and he had no plan B.

***

Hampton and Gillis had a small office above a stationer's in a side road that led off the lower High Street. He pressed the doorbell and climbed the narrow stairs to the first floor. Directly opposite the top of the stairs was a half-glazed door with 'Hampton & Gillis, Discrete Investigations' in gold leaf on the glass. Below it was a card inviting callers to 'Please Knock and Wait'. He knocked on the glass and a voice called, "Come in." He opened the door and found himself in a small but tidy room with a desk facing the door with two chairs in front of it and a large swivel chair behind in which sat a middle-aged man with a well-trimmed moustache and gold rimless glasses. He stood and shook hands with his visitor and pointed to one of the chairs. "Good morning, Sir, please take a seat. I'm Frank Gillis, and you must be Mr. Thompson?"

His visitor nodded, "Yes, Alan Thompson."

"If you would just give me a rough idea of your requirements, Sir, then I'll run through our terms, etc. with you and our fees of course."

"Fine. It is a fairly simple matter, at least I hope that it will be for you. I'm given to believe that a young man was brought into the A&E with a serious leg injury last Tuesday evening, although I do not know which hospital that was. I just want to know his name and address and which hospital he is in, and, hopefully, the ward."

"And may I ask why you need to know this, Sir?"

"I think it is possible that he may be my nephew. I haven't been able to contact him for a while and I'm getting worried. He lives on his own you see."

"You could just ring the hospital, Sir, and ask if he has been admitted. They may not give you much information, but they would confirm if someone of that name was a patient."

"Ah, well this is a little embarrassing actually. For reasons that I need not go into at the moment, he doesn't always use his own name. I have known him use at least three different ones when the mood takes him, and I thought it might sound odd to the Hospitals if I was enquiring after someone but seemed not to know their name. Do you follow me?"

Gillis pursed his lips and frowned slightly, "Hmm, yes, I think perhaps I do. I could, of course, make a few phone calls on your behalf, although that might not work if there is anything, er, shall we say 'unorthodox' about his circumstances? Do you think there might be, Mr. Thompson?"

"I have no idea, that is why I want to know who he is. If he is not my nephew then I don't really care who he is, or what he has done, if anything."

"Right, Mr. Thompson, let me just explain our terms and fees to you then, if you find them satisfactory, we can take it from there. I could make a few phone calls whilst you are here and that may be all it takes, otherwise we will need to, shall we say, explore other possibilities. How does that sound?"

Thompson agreed and Gillis ran through his spiel, then pulled a sheet of paper from his desk drawer headed 'Contract of Service'. "Can we just get the formalities out of the way?"

Alan Thompson took four twenty-pound notes from his wallet and dropped them on the desk. "Why don't you try the phone calls first?" he asked. "Then if that works, we'll have no need for any paperwork, OK?"

Gillis gave a slight smile and picked up his phone. He pointed to a coffee machine in the corner of the office and said, "Help yourself to a coffee, Mr. Thompson, it's not the best in the world but most people find it drinkable."

"Thank you, but I'm fine for now." He noted that Gillis seemed to have the hospital switch-board number stored in his phone and was waiting for it to answer. He then introduced himself and explained that he was trying to trace a missing person who may have been brought into A&E three evening ago, which would be last Tuesday. He listened for a few moments, then said, "Yes, of course, I completely understand, but could you perhaps put me through to the ward?"

He listened again, then spoke again. After what seemed an age, he replaced the phone and looked at his client. "They were very reluctant to give me any information at all but there was a young man admitted to Elmington General with a leg injury last Tuesday evening. They will not give his name or where he is, although I suspect it will be trauma and orthopaedic which is

Bolton Ward. I'm afraid that is the best I can do – on the phone, that is."

"What do you suggest, then?"

"Well, you could walk round the ward during their visiting hours to see if you recognize your nephew, although if he is in a single room that might not work."

"I have a suggestion," said Thompson, "that could be worth a try if you are prepared to go along with it?"

"Try me."

Thompson placed a small card on the desk and explained what he had in mind. Gillis frowned and sucked in his breath. "Oh, I'm not sure about that, Sir. That would be highly irregular."

"Really? Why?"

"Well," he paused. "It would be unethical to say the least."

"Perhaps innovative might be a better description," said Thompson, "and profitable of course, hmm?"

Gillis picked up the card that Thompson had put on the desk. "This photograph doesn't look a bit like me."

"Of course, it doesn't, I have only just met you. But I have never yet seen an identity or passport photo that looks remotely like the person to whom it belongs so I doubt if that would matter. And in any case, who is likely to examine it that carefully?"

Gillis's eyes hardened. "You really want to know who this man is, don't you?"

"That's why I'm here. Of course, if you think it beyond your capabilities or anything I can always try someone else although you struck me as a resourceful type who would not be adverse to a little creative activity as a change from, perhaps, tailing errant husbands."

Gillis smiled. "Possibly so, but this sort of 'creative activity' as you call it could not go through my books as described, and it would naturally attract a somewhat higher price than would tailing errant husbands."

"Certainly, shall we say half now and half on completion? Could you do it today?"

Gillis drew a desk diary towards him and opened it, being careful to hold it at such an angle that Thompson could not see the blank page. "No, I'm afraid not. I could manage tomorrow morning though if that would suit?"

When Thompson nodded his agreement, Gillis said, "How does four hundred pounds sound, Sir?"

"Excessive," said Thompson. "I was thinking more of two."

"Impossible. But I could come down to three-fifty perhaps."

"Three hundred and we have a deal."

They finally agreed on three hundred and thirty pounds, Thompson drew the money from his wallet and said, "I will call tomorrow at about twelve, will that suit?"

"If you give me your phone number, I will give you a ring, save you a journey?"

"I will need to come in to pick up a copy of the photograph that you will have, won't I? So, I will call tomorrow at about twelve. Agreed?"

"Agreed," said Gillis as he picked up the money and slipped it into his pocket. "Until tomorrow, then."

Eleven

Visiting hours in Bolton Ward were from two p.m. to four, and from six to eight. At just after two p.m., a woman of about forty with bright red-dyed hair and piercings through her ears, upper lip and nose, strode into the ward and approached the nurses' station. She rapped on the counter with long fingers smothered in cheap rings and glared at the nurse who was talking on the phone. "Where's Denton?" she snapped.

The nurse put her hand over the phone mouthpiece and said, "I'm sorry, Madam, who are you?"

"I'm 'is mother, where is he?"

"He is in a private room, Madam, but I'm afraid he is not allowed any visitors at the moment."

"Balls! I'm his mother and I wants to see 'im."

"As I just said, Madam, that will not be possible. Perhaps you would like to speak to the sister in charge of the ward – I'll see if she is free if you like."

"No. I don't like. I just want to see my son, now, which room is he in?"

The woman looked around the ward and saw P.C. Carter outside a door to what was obviously a side room. "Don't bovver yourself, kid, I can see it." She walked towards the door and Carter moved so that he was directly in front of her. "I'm sorry, Madam, but you can't go in there."

"Why? What's the little sod done now?"

The Sister had heard the commotion and reached the door

just after Denton's mother. "I'm Sister Wilson, what appears to be the trouble here?"

"I'm 'Arry Denton's mother and I wants to see `im. And I wants to see `im *now*."

"And I have just told the lady that she can't," said Carter.

The Sister looked at Carter and said, "Maybe just for a moment or two, George? After all she *is* his mother."

"It wouldn't matter if she was Mother Superior," said Carter, "my orders are quite definite. No one goes in, and that means no one."

"We'll see about that," snarled the woman. "I'll speak to your Boss, who is he?"

"You do that by all means, Madam. You can ask for Sergeant Manners or Chief Inspector Parker at County Police Headquarters."

"And don't you think I won't. You ain't 'eard the last of this, you bastard!" She pushed Carter in the chest, turned on her heels and stormed out of the ward, slamming the door behind her as she went.

Carter looked at the Sister, and shook his head. "Makes you feel almost sorry for him with a mother like that, doesn't it?"

Sister Wilson smiled at him. "Oh, no, Constable, I couldn't possibly comment on that."

Carter chuckled and resumed his seat.

Twelve

The man who had introduced himself to Frank Gillis as Alan Thompson had already made several purchases in a variety of shops in the town before he entered the larger of the town's two fancy dress shops. He browsed for a while but could find nothing on his list. He looked around and spotted a young man whom he rightly assumed to be the manager. "I wonder if you could help me, please?"

"I will do my very best, Sir, what is it that you are looking for?"

"Well," said Thompson, "I'm going to a fancy dress dance with my local dance club and the theme is 'doctors and nurses'. My daughter insists that I do not go as a nurse with a sexy short skirt, which was obviously my first choice, and I have to admit that I don't really have the legs for fishnet tights, so I'm looking for a doctor outfit. I don't have the figure for blue scrubs and clogs either, so I'm looking for a white lab coat and a toy stethoscope, and perhaps something to pad my body out a bit. Any ideas?"

"You might just be in luck there, I think I have a white coat out in the storeroom and there are some stethoscopes on the rack behind you, but they are for sale, not rent, I'm afraid – you never know where they might have been." He chuckled at his joke. "The false body padder is another thing, though; the only ones we keep are the muscular six-pack type, which are designed to be worn under a shirt open to waist rather than a white coat, but you could easily get one online, I'm sure."

"Ah, well, there's the snag you see. I don't have a computer or anything, and if I did, I wouldn't have a clue how to get something, er, in-line did you say?"

"Online, Sir. But I could help you there, do you have a phone?"

"No, I'm afraid not." He appeared to think for a moment and then said, "Look, this might be a dreadful imposition, but could you order one for me on your line thing? I would give you the money now and I could pop back and pick it up when you get it, and I would naturally not expect you to do it for nothing." He pulled his wallet out of his pocket and looked pleadingly at the manager. He had long ago discovered that putting on the 'useless old codger' act could be of great benefit, particularly in large stores and libraries etc. The manager looked at him and said, "Well, it would be highly irregular, and I couldn't use the shop computer, of course, but I suppose I could do it on my phone for you... but you would have to pay me now and it would have to be cash."

"That's absolutely no problem at all, you are a star. How soon could it be here do you think?"

"Possibly tomorrow with a bit of luck."

"It's a dreadful cheek, I know, but could we try the white coat that you have please, and if it doesn't fit, perhaps you could get one of those too?"

The manager fetched the coat which proved to be too small to wear a padded body under it. He tapped on his phone for a few minutes, then said, "A white lab coat is no problem and there are some padded 'body enhancers' which are a sort of foam material or there is an inflatable version. A bit more expensive, of course, but your choice, Sir. And you are in luck too, they will both be here on Monday if we order them right away."

"That is wonderful," said Thompson, "I think the inflatable one sounds ideal. It's only for the one dance, of course, but we all like to make an effort."

"Then if you are sure, Sir, I will order them now. Better leave it to the late afternoon on Monday to collect them just to be on the safe side, though. So let me put the stethoscope through the till for you, and then the online order will be a total of seventy-nine."

Thompson paid for the till, then gave the manager one hundred pounds and waved away his protest. "Oh, by the way, who do I ask for? I didn't ask your name."

"Sorry, Sir, I'm Jamie Norris, manager of this emporium, for my sins."

Thompson shook his hand and thanked him, agreeing to return on the Monday afternoon.

Thirteen

Frank Gillis was wearing a linen jacket with an apparent NHS identity badge clipped to the breast pocket which proclaimed him to be Roger Newman BPharm, pharmacist, and carrying a clip board with a few papers on it, when he entered Bolton Ward at about eleven o'clock the next morning. He had chosen his time well, the morning doctor's rounds were over, the hot drinks trolley had been returned to its store and there was a relatively quiet spell before the lunches would appear. He nodded at the nurse who was relaxing at the nurses' station and said, "Pharmacy, how many new admissions?"

"Just two," replied the Nurse, "room one, with the rather dishy copper on the door, and bed six, Mr. Beavis, a builder who was working on some scaffolding and found that sadly he couldn't fly after all, and broke his shoulder when he hit the ground. But don't you dare repeat that!"

Gillis grinned and walked over to the door that was protected by the 'dishy copper'. "Roger Newman," he said, waggling the badge hanging from his pocket, "I'm from the pharmacy, just checking on the medication requirements for the new admissions."

P.C. Carter opened the door for him, and because he hadn't seen him before, stood at the open door while Gillis nodded to Denton. "Good morning, Sir, I'm from the pharmacy, I just need to check the medication that has been prescribed for you to make sure we have enough in stock for your needs." He took Denton's records from the holder at the bottom of his bed and while appearing to study the contents and make an entry into his phone, he took a picture of Denton's identity label and then took another of Denton's face. He replaced the records in their holder and turned to the door. "Thank you, Sir." He crossed the ward to bed six and repeated the charade, then left the ward with a cheery wave to the nurse. "See you again, be good."

***

Later on that Monday afternoon, Mr. Thompson returned to the Fancy Dress shop. He could not see Jamie Norris, so he called to a shop assistant, introduced himself and asked if the Manager was about. "I'm sorry, Sir, he has just been called over to our other branch at Saddleton. But he has left a package for you and told me to wish you every success at your 'do'."

"Thank you very much, and please thank Jamie for me when he returns." He left the shop with his parcel, then made his way to Frank Gillis' office. He climbed the stairs again and knocked on the door which he opened in response to the grunted, "Come in."

"Good afternoon, Mr. Gillis, how did your little adventure go? Successful, I hope."

"Surprisingly so, Mr. Thompson. Nerve wracking to the extreme I must say, but, yes, successful."

"Good, then please tell me."

Gillis laid two photographs on the table, one of the identity label, and the other a full face of Denton. Mr. Thompson picked them up and scrutinised them carefully. "Oh, good, that isn't Johnny. What a relief." He smiled at Gillis. "You've no idea how glad I am."

Gillis looked at him, "You are quite sure, Sir?"

"Oh, absolutely, he's nothing like Johnny. Of course, that means I still don't know where the little bugger is, but at least he's not in hospital, creating mayhem among the nurses. I am so grateful to you, Frank."

He passed across the balance of the bill with an extra ten pounds, shook hands and left.

Fourteen

At just before eight o'clock that evening, P.C. Tony Walters went into Bolton Ward and tried to introduce himself to the charge nurse who had just come on duty and was busy with the 'hand-over' routine with the day shift nurses. He went over to George Carter who was standing outside the door of Denton's room. "All OK, George?"

"Yeah, boring as hell, though. I've had more excitement watching paint dry. I hope you've brought a good book with you?"

Walters tapped his pocket. "E-book, mate, with about fifty or so books on it and never a police procedural among 'em."

"Oh, all Enid Blyton, is it?"

The charge nurse interrupted them. "Sorry about that, chaps, but the hand-over is never a good time. I'm Jacob Odubi, and I'm in charge of the night shift."

"Tony Walters, and I've just relieved George here so he can go home and play. My shift is a short one tonight, I'm due to be relieved at two a.m., but I'll try not to wake you when I go."

"Bloody cheek!" grinned Odubi. "And that's no way to ensure a supply of coffee through the wee small hours."

"Well, I've heard reports about the coffee here, and I'm not sure that the threat to withhold it is as frightening as you think."

"OK, so I'll just have to think of something else, then. Meanwhile, I can't stand here wasting your time; I have patients to annoy. I'll catch up with you later."

George Carter punched Odubi gently on the shoulder and said, "Well, just make sure you keep annoying this fella – I'm off."

Walters opened the door to Denton's room, glanced inside, then closed the door and sat on the chair. He watched the nurses for a while as they visited each patient in turn, then after ten minutes or so Jacob returned and entered Denton's room carrying two replacement drip bags which he hung on the frame over the bed, and connected them both to the cannula in Denton's arm. He adjusted the flow of each, then, satisfied, picked up the used bags, exchanged a few words with Denton and left the room, closing the door behind him.

"How do you take your coffee, Tony?"

"As often as I can, Jacob. And white with two sugars, please."

"Got it, black with no sugar, OK."

Walters grinned and shook his fist at Jacob. He sat for a few more minutes, then, when the initial burst of activity among the nurses had subsided and most of them seemed to disappear, he took his e-reader from his pocket and settled back for a quiet, if boring, few hours.

Fifteen

At about nine o'clock, a tall, stocky man in a white coat came into the ward and stopped in front of the large board that hung on the wall of the corridor. It showed the names of all the patients, their bed number and the name of the Consultant in charge of their care, the estimated date of discharge and several sets of letters and numbers which meant nothing to him. He nodded with satisfaction when he saw that H Denton was in room one, was under the care of Mr. Connaught, and that there was no date entered for his estimated discharge. He took a pair of blue sterile gloves from a rack on the wall next to the notice board and snapped them on. He adjusted the stethoscope in his pocket so that it protruded slightly and looked around for a nurse. He saw a bank nurse at the nurses' station and went towards her, adjusting his face mask. "Good evening, nurse, I'm Alec Sinclair. Mr. Connaught has asked me to pop in and have a look at Mr. Denton. I am not usually on his team; I normally work in City Royal but I've been seconded here for a few days – staff shortages affect us all, apparently."

The nurse said, "He is in room one, Sir, I'll come with you."

"That won't be necessary my dear, I won't be more than a few minutes."

"Well, if you are sure, Sir."

"Of course." He went towards P.C. Walters who, he was sure, had overheard everything he had said. Walters stood up, ready to open the door. "Dr. Sinclair, did you say, Sir?"

"No. *Mr.* Sinclair. Physicians are Doctor, Surgeons are Mr."

"Oh, I'm sorry, Sir, no offence meant."

"None taken, Constable. Now, I just need a wee check on Mr. Denton. I understand that he has been complaining about his pain, so we must see what we can do for him, hmm?" He made sure that Walters got a glimpse of the identity tag that was clipped to his breast pocket, then nodded at the door. Walters opened it for him, and he went in, closing the door behind him. Walters made an entry in his pocketbook; he noted that Mr Alec Sinclair MBBS FRCS and something was about five-foot-ten, of stocky build, with brown hair going grey at the sides, spoke with a slight but noticeable Scottish burr and had rather striking blue eyes. He put a question mark against the brown hair, suspecting that it was dyed. He knew for a fact that his father-in-law dyed his hair and Mr. Sinclair's had a similar look. Not that it mattered, of course, but even so...

The door had a glass viewing panel at the top which comprised two sheets of glass with a narrow-slatted venetian blind sandwiched between them that could be controlled by a knob at the bottom. Sinclair closed the blind and locked the door. He then switched on the light above the bed and said, "Good evening, Mr. Denton, I am Mr. Sinclair, and I have just popped in to see how you are getting along. Could you just confirm your date of birth for me, please?"

Denton scowled at him and mumbled his date of birth.

"Fine, now let's have a little look at this leg, shall we?" He pulled the sheet back and put his gloved hand on Denton's ankle. "Any pain there?"

"No, it's the bleedin' knee, ain't it?"

Sinclair put his hand on the leg just below the knee and pressed hard. Denton squealed and gasped. "Aw, fer crissakes doc, that 'urt."

"OK, I think I will give you a shot of a little more potent painkiller, then, can't have you suffering like that, can we?"

He rolled the bedside table away from the bed and stood with his back to Denton. He took two needleless syringes from his pocket and placed them on the table. There was a jug of water and a glass on the table, so he picked up the smaller of the two syringes and, dipping the end in the jug, drew a small amount of water into it. He disconnected one of the intravenous drip bags from the cannula and screwed the syringe into it. "This may feel a little cold as it goes in, Sir. He depressed the plunger slowly whilst watching Denton's face. "OK, Sir?" he asked.

Denton nodded, "Yeah, I s'pose."

"Good."

Sinclair moved closer to Denton and pulled the sheet back up over is arm and tucked it firmly under the mattress. He reached for the bed controller and lowered the head as far as it would go, then, with one quick move, he clamped his gloved hand over Denton's mouth. Denton stared at him in puzzlement and fear and tried to move his arm, but it was held tight by the sheet.

Sinclair pushed Denton's head down hard against the pillow and leaned close to his face. "Now, I want you to stay quiet and listen very, very carefully to what I say." Sweat started to form on Denton's forehead and he tried to struggle.

"Listen to me, *Mister* Denton, this is very important. What I have just injected into you is not a painkiller." Denton frowned, his eyes betraying confusion and fear.

"No, not a painkiller at all, but a very potent nerve agent. A military-grade nerve agent, actually, and unless I inject the antidote which, luckily for you, I have here, within ten minutes, you will die the most horrific death imaginable. Do you understand what I am saying?"

Denton nodded frantically, he forehead now streaming with sweat and a wet patch forming between his legs.

"Good, good. Because I am going to ask you some questions now and if you answer them truthfully, I will inject the antidote and you will live. You may feel a little uncomfortable for a short while, but you will live. If you refuse to answer, or tell me any porkies, then I will just walk away and within…" he glanced at his watch, "within eight minutes you will be dead. Got it? And it will do no good calling the staff here, because even if they knew which nerve agent I have used, and in the unlikely event that they would have the antidote here, by the time they got it to you I'm afraid your…" he looked at his watch again, "your seven-and-a-half minutes would be long gone."

He took his mobile phone from his pocket and held it close to Denton's face. "Are you ready? Now, I want the names and addresses of your two mates that were with you when you attacked the old couple last Tuesday evening, and don't even think of lying to me."

He relaxed his hand slightly from Denton's mouth. "Come on, then, who were they?"

Denton struggled to speak, then croaked, "Zack. Zack Peters was one."

"What does he look like?"

"Tall, skinny, wiv a long ponytail."

Sinclair nodded his approval. "His address?"

"I ain't sure of the number, but it's the first 'ouse after the bungalows on the right in 'adley Court Road."

"Does he have a car?"

Now that he had started to talk, he was desperate to please this nightmare of a man who held his life in his hands. "Nah, 'es got a motorbike. An old black Beesa, but I don't know the reg number, 'onest I don't."

"Beesa?"

"Yeah BSA."

"Right. And the other one?"

"That was Jacko. Well, that's what we calls 'im becos 'is name is Jacques. Cole."

"Cole? What sort of name is that?"

"Cole. It's Colin. Colin Jacques. He lives on the new estate, in Preston Way. Number thirty-four. An' 'e's gotta van, an old Ford transit, white, of course. It's a load of crap, an 'e leaves the keys in it 'oping someone will nick it, but I told 'im no one would nick it even if they missed the last bus."

"And what does Colin Jacques look like?"

"Big, bulky, gotta lotta tattoos and grey 'air"

"You are lying."

"No, I ain't, 'is 'air is grey but it ain't very long and it's a bit spikey and 'e usually wears a woolly beanie 'at."

Sinclair stood up and put his phone back in his pocket. "Now, that wasn't too difficult, was it? Thank you, I think you have earned that antidote now."

"Please, please an' I won't tell no one nuffin."

Sinclair picked up the larger of the two syringes and withdrew the plunger, then screwed it into the cannula and slowly depressed the plunger, forcing air into the vein. "This may feel a little uncomfortable for a while, but it will work." He unscrewed the syringe, withdrew the plunger, reconnected it and repeated the procedure, injecting a further syringe full of air, then reconnected the drip bag to the cannula. "Right, that's that, then. Now, it is important that you stay very still and quiet for at least five or ten minutes. You may possibly feel a little pain in the arm but that will soon pass." He opened the blinds on the door panel and switched off the bed light, then opened the door and went out.

P.C. Walters looked up. "Everything all right, Sir?"

"Oh, yes, Constable, he should be much more comfortable now. He may be a little restless for a while, but it is important that he should stay as quiet as possible. He will probably drop off shortly. I can't stay now, I have just been paged to go to A&E, bit of an emergency there, so I'll bid you goodnight."

"Goodnight, Sir."

As Sinclair walked towards the ward door, the bank nurse that he had spoken to when he arrived came out of one of the bays further along the corridor and hurried towards him. "Oh, Mr. Sinclair, I wonder of you could spare a minute to have a look at Mrs. Hepton, she has had a hip replacement and is in a lot of pain. Dr. Johnson said if it continued he would write up some morphine for her, but I wonder if you could do that for me please?"

"I am sorry, lassie, but I have just been paged to A&E urgently. You'll have to ring the duty houseman, I'm afraid." He walked quickly out of the door and looked around. Seeing that no one was around, he retrieved his brief case from where it was leaning against the wall behind an equipment trolley and carried it through a door marked 'Toilets. Staff and Patients only'.

A few minutes later, a much thinner man wearing a thin, grey fleece emerged and took the lift down to the ground floor, found his car and drove home.

As soon as he got home, he poured himself a glass of scotch, listened to Denton's answers on his phone and copied the relevant facts into his notebook, then deleted the recording. He nodded to himself and went upstairs. He stripped off and got into the shower where he vigorously shampooed his hair again and again until he was satisfied that he had removed all trace of the water-soluble colour mousse from his hair that he had applied previously.

He got into bed but could not sleep, visions of old motor bikes and unlocked vans kept him awake, until eventually an idea started to form. "Yes," he thought, "that might just work."

He had another plan.

Sixteen

Some time after Sinclair had left, Tony Walters was sitting in his chair, reading his e-book, when Jacob Odubi came up to him with a mug of coffee. "Oh, Jacob, you are star, thank you."

"You're welcome. Is everything OK?"

"I suppose so," he nodded to the door, "He was a bit noisy for a while, but he soon quietened down."

Jacob nodded and said, "Well I'd better just have a quick peep at him." He switched his torch on and opened the door and shone the torch towards Denton. Denton was on his back staring at the ceiling with unseeing eyes, bathed in sweat and his face twisted in a rictus of abject terror.

He turned the room light on and pressed the alarm button on the wall above the bed head. He called, "Tony, quick as you can, grab a phone, ring four two's and just say 'cardiac arrest, Bolton Ward, room one'. There's a phone on my desk." He pulled down the sheet and started to apply chest compressions.

Walters rushed to the nurses' station, snatched up the phone and pressed the two button four times. It was answered almost immediately, and he spoke rapidly, adding, needlessly, "It's urgent."

Within minutes, the ward door burst open, and the crash team rushed along the corridor, a doctor in blue scrubs and two nurses pushing the cardiac emergency trolley. Walters waved them towards the room, and the doctor spoke to Odubi as Jacob continued with the chest compressions and outlined the situation to the team. The doctor waved Walters away. "Out, out, we need room, here. And shut the door. Now."

Walters backed out of the room and closed the door but left it slightly ajar. He heard the doctor calling out some numbers and a response from one of the nurses, then he heard 'stand clear' and a thump. Silence. Then more numbers and what were obviously attempts to restart the heart were repeated a further twice. After several more minutes of murmured conversation, the nurses came out with the trolley, and, without a glance at Walters, left the ward.

The doctor and Odubi came out of the room, closed the door, and returned to the Nurses Station deep in quiet conversation. When there was a slight pause, Walters joined them and asked, "What's the situation then, Jacob?"

Odubi lowered his voice. "I'm afraid we couldn't save him, he was too far gone. We tried everything we could, but..." He shrugged.

"So, what happens now?"

"That is just what the doctor and I were discussing. Normally I would call Geordie, sorry, the mortuary attendant and he would come and collect him but..." He paused for a moment. "The doctor here is a little concerned."

The doctor was a small, wiry man with hair almost to his shoulders and dark framed glasses with a slight blue tint on the lenses. "Jon Reynolds. As Jacob here says, I am just a little concerned. This is rather unusual, you see, a twenty-three-year-old man with just a broken leg, albeit with some complications, but nevertheless, hardly a normal candidate for a massive cardiac arrest, or heart attack, as you would say. I would be happier if one of his care team had a look at him before we move him. Please don't misunderstand me, though, I have no doubt whatsoever that this was a cardiac arrest, and I am quite prepared to sign the necessary certification to that effect, but even so..." His voice trailed off.

Jacob Odubi said, "Let me see if any of Mr. Connaught's team are here. There is usually one, either on duty or 'on call'." He picked up the phone and spoke to the receptionist. "Oh, good, would you connect me to him then, please, and yes, it is very necessary." He rolled his eyes, then turned his head away from the phone and said, "We are in luck, Bob McGrath is on call. He will be in the restroom. Probably reading the Beano and praying for a quiet night. Ooh, language Mr. McGrath! I didn't expect you to hear that," he lied. "But seriously, Bob, I have Dr. Reynolds with me on Bolton. He is on the cardiac crash team that we just had to call for your Mr. Denton. I am afraid that, despite all our efforts, we couldn't save him, and we were wondering if-"

McGrath cut in. "What? He is, er, was, a twenty-three-year-old with a broken leg for Crissakes, how did he come by a heart attack?"

"Well, he certainly did Bob and Doctor Reynolds was hoping you might come and have a quick look at him before we let him go down into Geordie's tender care."

"I'll be with you in five."

Dr. Reynolds put his hand on Odubi's shoulder. "Thanks for that, Jacob"

Bob McGrath was as good as his word, and joined them in just under the five minutes. They all went into Denton's room, including Walters, who closed the door behind them. Odubi and Reynolds gave McGrath a detailed account of the events as he examined the body. He asked a few questions of Dr. Reynolds which meant nothing to Walters, but the answers obviously satisfied McGrath. "Well, I agree with you, Jon, it looks pretty clear cut. But why a cardiac arrest at twenty-three?" He looked at Walters. "I suppose you chaps didn't frighten him to death, did you?"

"I hope you are joking, Sir," replied Walters, "but as far as I understand, he had received a formal caution and had been told that he would be arrested on suspicion of GBH and/or manslaughter as soon as he was discharged from here. But he didn't seem too frightened to me. He was worried about it for sure, but as far as I can make out, he was just his usual unpleasant, arrogant self, but Sergeant Manners could tell you more about him than I can. I just sit outside the door."

"Thank you, Constable, I didn't mean that as it sounded, but a cardiac arrest can be brought on, in exceptional circumstances, by an attack of fear, and although his facial muscles have relaxed now, Dr. Reynolds said that his face was distorted with what he described as a look of terror when he first saw him. But again, that isn't necessarily unusual. If the victim suffers an acute pain in the chest, he might well look frightened." He turned to Odubi. "Jacob, I think that for the time being you should keep him here. I will have to talk to Mr. Connaught, he may well want to see him, or at least he will have some opinion on where we should go from here, and," he turned to Walters, "I'm sure that you will want to notify your Sergeant, er, Manners, was it?"

He shook hands with Reynolds. "Thank you, doctor, and thank you, Jacob, I will be in touch as soon as I have spoken to Mr. Connaught."

***

As Reynolds left the ward, Walters radioed in to Control, "824 Walters to Control, over." His radio crackled, then he said, "Can you connect me to DS Manners please?" He listened for a moment, then, "Oh, is he indeed? Well D.C. Lee or Chief Inspector Parker then, please. Yes, I do know what the time is, but Chief Inspector Parker will want to hear to what I have to report."

He explained the situation to Chief Inspector Parker who said, "If there is any suspicion about the death then you will remain where you are. We need to be a little careful; we cannot treat the room as a 'scene of crime' until we have more information, but you must ensure that it is not cleaned or disturbed in any way until we know one way or the other. It is Dave Manners' wedding anniversary, so he was out this evening with his family, but I will get him in the morning, first thing. In the meanwhile, make sure that you brief your relief."

***

Meanwhile Bob McGrath phoned Connaught. "I think you were right, Bob. I will get Margaret to arrange a meeting first thing in the morning. You can advise her as to who should attend, but I would like everyone there who might be able to add anything to the overall picture, then I will decide if we need an autopsy. I will ring her now, although I don't suppose that will please her at this time of night. I think you might expect a call from her shortly after that, so I suggest you give some thought as to who will need to attend." He hung up and checked his watch – nearly eleven p.m. "Oh, well, needs must."

It was several minutes before his secretary answered. "Margaret, it's Laurence here, you sound a little breathless, I hope I haven't disturbed you?"

"Don't even ask!"

"Oh, dear, then I am sorry," he chuckled, "perhaps I should call back in a couple of hours?"

"That isn't in the remotest bit funny, *Sir*."

"No, of course not, Margaret, and I am sorry, but I wouldn't have called you were it not important."

"I imagine that would be so, so what is the problem?"

"I would like you to get into the office early tomorrow, and try and book a meeting room for me, not too big, perhaps for about half-a-dozen or so. And as early as possible, say eight-thirty-ish. If you ring Bob, he is on call at the General tonight, he will give you a list of those I would like to be there. Then I would like you to ring them and ask them to attend. You can give them the actual venue in the morning as soon as you have it booked. Ask them, but do not accept 'no' for an answer. And I would like you there as well, of course, to take notes for me."

"Ring them? At this time of night, Sir?"

"Yes, as soon as you can. A few of them will be on night duty and we need to catch them before they go off."

"Right, but what is this about, then?"

"Oh, of course, I'm sorry. One of our patients died a little earlier this evening and the doctor on the crash team spoke to Bob and they are both a little concerned about the circumstances. I need to get as much information as I can so that I can decide if I need to order an autopsy."

"OK, Laurence, I'll get onto it straight away."

"Bless you, Margaret, I will see you in the office at about seven-thirty, then."

"Oh, you do mean early! OK, 7.30 then, goodnight."

"Goodnight."

Margaret rang Bob McGrath. "Ah, I do believe it is the secretarial night shift. The Bow warned me that you would call,"

"The Bow? Robert!" she said with mock severity. "How many times have I told you to have a little more respect for your Lord and Master?"

"Oh, I respect my Lord and Master, madam, it's just his eye-watering taste in bow ties that I find hard to stomach."

"I can't think what you mean, Robert. Have you no sense of fashion? Or of the aesthetic pleasures that such things can bestow on an otherwise drab and weary world?"

"I shall refuse to answer that on the grounds that it might incriminate me, or I plead the fifth, as our Colonial Cousins might say."

"But enough of this badinage, let us to business. What is this list you have for me?"

He read out the list that he had prepared, with the internal phone numbers for the hospital staff, but said, "When you call Sergeant Manners, I suggest you ask him if any of his colleagues should also attend, and he will have to contact the coppers that were 'on the door' as they put it."

She thanked him and began to work through the list, choosing those who were already at the hospital first, and apologising that their night shift was going to be extended somewhat. It was well over an hour before she had finished. She went back into her bedroom where her husband was gently snoring. He woke up as she got back into bed. "Oh, hello stranger, where have you been all my life?"

"Don't get any ideas, sugar-pops, I have to be up and away disgustingly early in the morning, so just go back to sleepy-byes like a good boy."

Seventeen

At exactly eight-thirty the following morning, Laurence Connaught entered the meeting room and took his seat at the head of a long, polished oak table around which were seated everyone that Bob McGrath had asked to be there. Bob glanced at the bright gold bow tie with multi-coloured electric flashes running diagonally across it. He looked at Margaret, raised his eyebrows and rolled his eyes. She frowned at him but had difficulty suppressing a smile. She placed a small digital recorder on the table and held a pencil poised over a notebook balanced on her knee.

"Good morning, gentlemen, and lady. Before we start, I would like to thank all of you for making the effort to attend here at such short notice. And I would say that I appreciate your courtesy in wearing face coverings, however, as you know, the restrictions covering that have been relaxed and I would be quite happy if those of you who so wish should remove your masks. In fact, it might be preferable, in order that we better hear and understand what might be said here. I realise that some of you have already spent a full night on duty and that I am keeping you from your beds, and I apologise for that. This is an informal meeting, not in any way an inquest or an enquiry, but it is one which I felt necessary. And its purpose is as follows: As you will know, one of our patients, Mr. Harry Denton, died last evening, and I wish to apprise myself of the events concerning, and possibly preceding, his death so that I can decide whether or not to order an Autopsy to be held.

"Before we start any discussion, I think it would be of benefit if we each introduce ourselves. As you probably know, I am Laurence Connaught, and I am the senior orthopaedic consultant here at Elmington General, and the lady on my right is my private secretary, Margaret Yates, whom I have asked to be here to take notes. I should add perhaps that, as you will have noticed, she has placed a small recording device on the table, purely for convenience, I assure you, nothing sinister. Perhaps we can now go round the table with our introductions? Bob?"

"I'm Bob McGrath, orthopaedic surgeon and registrar to Mr. Connaught."

"I am Jon Reynolds, and I was duty doctor on the cardiac emergency team that attended the call to Mr. Denton in Bolton Ward last evening."

"I am Alan Johnson, Senior Houseman on Bolton Ward. I was not on duty last evening, but I am here to answer any questions relating to Mr. Denton's general health and the treatment that he was undergoing here."

"I am charge nurse Jacob Odubi. I was in charge of Bolton Ward at the time, and it was I who discovered Mr. Denton in an apparent state of distress and initiated the emergency cardiac arrest alarm."

"P.C. Tony Walters. I was on duty yesterday evening in Bolton Ward, stationed outside room one. My duty was to prevent anyone other than medical staff from entering the room and also to prevent Mr. Denton from leaving if he should choose to try. I was on a split shift from eight p.m. until two a.m. this morning."

"P.C. George Carter. I had the same remit as P.C. Walters, and I was relieved by him at eight p.m. I am here because Chief

Inspector Parker thought there might be events that occurred before eight p.m. that could be relevant."

"I am Detective Sergeant David Manners, County CID. I have been investigating the possible, or I should say probable, involvement of Mr. Denton in a mugging which took place last Tuesday evening and which resulted in the unfortunate death of one of the victims, a Mrs. Mary Fleming."

"And I am Detective Chief Inspector Reg Parker, County CID. I am the senior investigating officer on the case to which Sergeant Manners has just referred, although all the interviews with Mr. Denton have been conducted by Sergeant Manners and D.C. Lee, another of my officers."

Connaught had been watching each man's face as they introduced themselves. "Thank you very much. Now, Mr. Odubi, you say that you raised the alarm, can you give us a little more detail please?"

"Yes, Sir. I looked in on Mr. Denton at a few minutes past nine in order to check on him and realised immediately that there was a problem. Although I said that he appeared to be in a distressed state, I am almost certain that he was already dead when I entered the room. I immediately commenced chest compressions and CPR and told P.C. Walters to ring the emergency number and report a cardiac arrest. Mr. Denton was on his back, his eyes were open and he was bathed in sweat. I got no response from him at all, but I continued with the chest compressions until the crash team arrived, when Doctor Reynolds took over."

"Thank you, nurse, Doctor Reynolds?"

"The 'four two's' call was logged at twenty-one-oh-nine and I was in Bolton Ward with my team about two minutes after that. I agree with Jacob, er, Charge Nurse Odubi, in that he had every appearance of life being extinct, certainly when I arrived. I gave an injection of adrenalin and applied several electro-shocks but there was no response and at twenty-one-thirty-two I pronounced him to be dead."

"And how many, exactly, was 'several' electro-shocks, Doctor?" interrupted Connaught.

"I beg your pardon, Sir. I applied three in total, ranging in intensity from medium on the first, then maximum power on the subsequent two."

"Thank you, Doctor. I hope you will agree that we need to be precise in these matters."

"Of course, sir, that was remiss of me. As I told Mr. McGrath, I was as certain as I reasonably could be that he had suffered a massive cardiac arrest, but given his age and apparent otherwise good health, I felt it worth raising the matter with a member of your team before I allowed him to be removed from the Ward."

"And quite right too, Sir," said Connaught.

"Mr. Odubi and I discussed the situation," continued Reynolds, "and P.C. Walters was present during some of that discussion. We were able to contact Mr. McGrath who, fortuitously, happened to be on call at the time and he came straight to the Ward."

"Thank you, Doctor. Bob?"

"Yes, Charge Nurse Odubi rang me and told me of their concerns, and I immediately went to the Ward. I saw Mr. Denton, but performed only a perfunctory examination of him, visual mainly, and I agreed with Doctor Reynolds that it had every indication of a massive cardiac arrest. It is possibly worth recording that, although his facial muscles had relaxed somewhat by the time I saw him, Doctor Reynolds had remarked that there was an expression of terror on his face when he first saw him. I pointed out, largely for the benefit of the P.C. I must say, that an expression of fear is not uncommon if the victim had suffered severe chest pains immediately prior to the onset of an arrest."

"Thank you, Bob," said Connaught, "That all seems pretty clear and straight forward, but may we dwell for a moment on this expression of fear on which you remarked, Doctor Reynolds? I imagine that, as a cardiologist, that would be not unfamiliar to you, yet you obviously felt it to be of sufficient import to remark on it. Was it perhaps excessive? Or unusual in some way? What was it that made you feel that it was worthy of remark?"

"To be honest, Sir, I am not quite sure why. Certainly, an expression of fear is not unusual, as has been said, but there was something about his eyes. I think the term 'abject terror' may sound a little dramatic, but it would not be over-emphasising it, in my opinion."

"So how was his demeanour prior to this event? Mr. Odubi, Doctor Johnson?"

Doctor Johnson said, "I had not seen him since my rounds that morning but as far as I am aware, his demeanour hadn't changed at all during his time here. He was surly, arrogant and thoroughly unpleasant right from the start. When he was first brought into the Ward from recovery, he refused to give any details about himself, even his name, which led me to believe that he had something to hide, which was of course borne out by Sergeant Manners' subsequent interest in him. In fact, Sister Grant asked me to intervene because he was becoming aggressive to the nurses and totally unco-operative when they were trying to get his details."

"And you were able to encourage him to co-operate?"

"Well, I wouldn't say co-operate exactly, but he did give his name and address eventually and enough details to enable his medical history to be determined."

"Thank you, Doctor Johnson, I won't embarrass you by asking how you might have achieved that."

Manners cut in, "I think that Doctor Johnson described Denton's attitude perfectly Sir. D.C. Lee and I interviewed him on a couple of occasions and had no co-operation from him at all. Of course, our interest in him was different to yours, but even so." He shrugged.

"Thank you, Sergeant. Now, considering his, shall we say mental state, prior to the apparent cardiac arrest, do you think it possible that your interviews with him might have induced this, um, apparent terror, of which doctor Reynolds has remarked?"

"Highly unlikely I would say, Sir. When D.C. Lee and I saw him following the death of Mrs. Fleming I cautioned him formally, and during that interview I told him that he would be arrested on suspicion of attempted robbery and assault causing actual bodily harm and possibly of manslaughter as soon as he was discharged from this hospital. And although he was obviously scared his response was as arrogant as ever and he refused to make any further comment. He certainly seemed worried when we mentioned manslaughter, but his reaction was a long way short of 'terror'."

"Thank you," said Connaught, "and are you aware, Mr. Odubi, of anything that occurred that might have been of some significance?"

"Nothing of which I am aware, Sir, but I was busy in one of the bays at the other end of the Ward for quite some time prior to that. It was only when I brought a mug of coffee for P.C. Walters that these events, er, unfolded, as it were."

"Constable Walters, can you shed any light on this?"

"I am not sure that I can, Sir, everything seemed fine when the doctor left. He had warned me of course that Mr. Denton might be a little uncomfortable for a while but that would soon pass. And, yes there were some noises for a while but as he had said, it soon went quiet."

Connaught looked at Johnson. "But you said that you had not seen him since the morning!"

"On no, Sir," said Walters, "not Doctor Johnson. It was Mr. Sinclair."

"Sinclair? Not Alec Sinclair?"

Walters turned the pages of his notebook, "Yes indeed, Sir. It was Mr., he corrected me for calling him 'Doctor', and explained that physicians were called 'Doctor', but Surgeons were always 'Mister'." He glanced at his notebook. "According to his identity tag, he was Mr Alec Sinclair MBBS FRCS bracket E-something."

"Alec?" interrupted Connaught. "What the devil was Alec doing here? He is at City Royal, surely."

"He said that he had been asked by you, Sir, er, by Mr. Connaught, to pop in and have a look at Mr. Denton. He did tell the nurse that he usually worked at City Royal but had been seconded here for a few days, quoting staff shortages."

Connaught frowned, "Do you know anything about this Bob?"

"No, Sir, it's news to me, we are no shorter of staff now than we usually are and a secondment like that would have had to have been authorised, or at least requested, by yourself."

"Well, check it with him, will you?"

"Of course." Bob took his phone from his pocket and moved into a corner of the room.

Connaught looked at Walters. "Did anyone else go into Mr.

Denton's room?"

Walters looked a little uncomfortable. "Absolutely not, Sir. My instructions were that no one other than medical staff should be allowed in, and no one was. At least not on any of my shifts."

Connaught looked at George Carter. "Constable?"

"And no one on any of my shifts, Sir. There was only one attempt, and that was a woman who said she was Denton's mother. I refused to let her in, much to her annoyance and she became quite abusive. She cast aspersions on my parentage and even threatened me with the wrath of Chief Inspector Parker!"

Parker chipped in, "Yes, I did indeed receive a phone call from the, er, lady who was, as P.C. Carter has inferred, somewhat distraught and totally unreasonable."

Bob McGrath returned to his seat. "Well, it certainly wasn't Alec, Sir. Apparently, his mother-in-law is very sick and he is on a week's leave, somewhere in the Cairngorms I believe. An errand of mercy rather than a holiday, I'm sure."

"Well, if this was an imposter, and it sounds very likely to be so, how would he know of Alec, and indeed, that he usually works at City Royal."

"That would be no problem at all," said Parker, "all one needs to do is to google 'orthopaedic surgeons' and there would be a list as long as your arm. Complete with their qualifications, specialities, and even their fees."

"Oh, yes, of course!" said Connaught. "I also am on that list. It does indeed contain a lot of details of one's qualifications, specialities and even education to some extent, almost one's CV in fact but no physical description other than a head and shoulders picture. Can you describe him for us Mr., er Constable, not that it is my concern, more in Chief Inspector Parker's remit of course but..."

Walters again referred to his notebook, more for effect than necessity. "He would be about five-foot-ten, quite stocky and spoke with a slight, but noticeable, Scottish burr. He had brown hair, grey at the sides and it was parted in the middle and slicked down. And, and this is just an impression, I suspect that his hair was dyed."

"And did no one go into the room with him?"

"No, Sir. I believe that the nurse offered to accompany him, but he declined, saying that would not be necessary as he would be only a few minutes."

"And would that be considered normal practice, Mr. Odubi."

"It would depend on the circumstances, Sir. In this case, of course, it was an apparent consultant that she was talking to, and, as I'm sure you know, Consultants are deeply revered and are unlikely to be challenged by a nurse. She would have expected him either to write up some additional medication or, if he thought that an analgesic injection more appropriate, he would prescribe that on the patient's notes then get the senior nurse, either Sister or Charge Nurse, to draw some from the ward drugs locker and then accompany him back to the patient where they would both verify that the medication was as prescribed before administering it. So, as he seemed not to have anything with him, in the way of drugs, it would be quite acceptable for her to act as she did."

"Deeply revered? What on earth do you mean, deeply revered?"

All the other doctors round the table suddenly seemed to find that the pattern of the wood grain on the top of the table totally absorbing and one or two shoulders were quietly shaking.

"Well, perhaps I should say 'highly esteemed', and in some cases possibly even a little awe inspiring."

"What utter nonsense, man. Well, where is this nurse? Have we heard any evidence from her?"

"There were two nurses and an HCA on duty with me last night. Both of them were bank nurses." He turned to the policemen and added, "Bank Nurses are stand-ins and are provided by a local Nursing Agency. We use them frequently, especially as this COVID pandemic has resulted in so many of our regular staff being off sick."

"Thank you for that, Mr. Odubi, I accept your reasoning for him to be allowed in unaccompanied, but I imagine that the Chief Inspector may want to question the nurse. Can you identify her for him?"

"Yes, of course. I am not sure which of the two it would have been that he spoke to, though, perhaps Constable Walters could help us there?"

Walters said, "I don't know her name, the identity tags that the agency nurses wear have their name of course but it is usually so small that it is impossible to read at a distance. However, I can say that she was very short, she had exceptionally dark hair and was of Asian appearance. I would hazard a guess as probably a Filipino?"

"Ah, thank you, that would be Annita, then. I can get her address from the ward records for you if you wish?"

Parker said, "I would be grateful if you would do that and ring either myself or Sergeant Manners as soon as you have it."

"Right, then," interjected Connaught, "now to get back to this imposter and the length of time that he was, um, *alone* with Mr. Denton. How long would you say that might have been, Constable?!"

"I would say no more than five minutes, six at the most."

"Well thank you all for your contributions, Gentlemen. This

all sounds highly irregular, and I will have no hesitation now in ordering an autopsy to be performed as soon as possible. I will of course have a copy of the report sent to you, Sir," he said to Parker.

"I assume then, Sir, that you consider this to be a suspicious death, in which case I must insist that the room is locked and that no one at all is to be admitted before I have arranged for a SOCO and a Forensic Team to examine it. It is now formally classified as a crime scene until it is proven otherwise."

"SOCO?" queried Connaught.

"I beg your pardon, Sir, jargon, I'm afraid, it means scene of crime officer. He, or she, will establish control of the area and will be entirely responsible for it. I must add that it will be necessary for all personnel who would normally have had access to the room, whether they be medical or auxiliary staff, to be fingerprinted without delay. For elimination purposes of course."

Odubi said, "Is that really necessary Chief Inspector, we are desperately short of beds you know."

"I'm sure you are, Nurse, and I'm sorry, but from what I have heard here, I have no doubt that this is indeed a suspicious death and although I won't presume the outcome of any autopsy findings, this could possibly develop into a murder investigation with all that that would entail. And speaking of the autopsy, Mr. Connaught, perhaps that could be conducted by our police pathologist?"

"I don't think that will be necessary," said Connaught coldly, "we have a perfectly competent pathologist here on site. You may, if you wish, attend as an observer, or appoint someone to attend in your place but the procedure will be conducted by our man. You will, naturally, be furnished with a full and unredacted copy of his report as soon as it becomes available. Now, does anyone have anything else to add? No? Then thank you all for your time. I rather suspect that the Chief Inspector may have some more questions for some of you, but at the moment that is all. Please avail yourselves of the dubious delights of the coffee machine in the corner." He gathered his papers together and beckoned McGrath and Margaret to follow him as he left the room.

***

Once back in his office, Connaught turned to Bob McGrath and said, "What was all that nonsense about 'deeply revered' and 'awe-inspiring'?"

"I've no idea," said Bob, "perhaps he'd just heard that old joke about Consultants?"

"Old joke? What old joke?"

"Oh, I wouldn't know, I'm sure."

"Tell me the 'old joke' Robert, and if there is any mention of bow ties, I will be looking for a replacement registrar by lunch-time."

"Bow ties, Sir? What could possibly be funny about bow ties?"

"The joke, Robert!"

"Well, of course, I don't know, but it could be the old one about the difference between God and a consultant."

"And just what, pray, is the difference?"

"God doesn't think he's a consultant. *Sir*."

"Oh, is that hairy old chestnut still doing the rounds? I thought that had passed its sell-by date decades ago."

"As I said, sir, I wouldn't know, and I don't think it's very funny, anyway. After all, I might be a consultant myself one day."

"Yes, and, Mr. McGrath, you are probably the world's worse

liar."

"Oh, he tries his best though," grinned Margaret.

"Don't encourage him, Margaret!"

Bob's pager buzzed in his pocket. "Excuse me." He indicated the phone on Connaught's desk. "May I?"

"Of course."

"McGrath. Yes. When? What analgesia? Has he been X-rayed? Well would you arrange that now please? Yes, I'll be right there." He hung up then said, "A&E, Sir, a young motor-cyclist has just had an argument with a lorry and appears to have come off second-best. I must go."

"Saved by the bell," grinned Connaught, "don't let us keep you then. As an aspiring deity I'm sure you'll cope, but if you need me, I'm free until the two p.m. fracture clinic and even then, I could get Freda to cover that for us."

McGrath thanked him and left the office.

Connaught grinned at Margaret and said, "You know, I have been extraordinarily lucky with my choice of registrars." He fingered his tie. "Despite Bob's pathetic lack of appreciation of the finer points of sartorial elegance."

Margaret frowned. "Lack of - whatever can you mean, Laurence?"

"Margaret, you are in danger of becoming as bad as he is!" His face became serious. "But to business, would you contact Ken Jessop and ask him if he could arrange a PM on our Mr. Denton as soon as possible please. Full toxicology, the lot. We need to know what caused that cardiac arrest and I suspect that the good Chief Inspector would like to know as soon we can possibly tell him." He ushered Margaret out and sat at his desk, shuffling the stack of papers that Margaret had brought in and shook his head sadly.

Eighteen

Manners nodded towards the door. "Yon Genius is a barrel of laughs, isn't he?"

"Well, he probably doesn't like his patients dying, at least not so soon after he's operated on them, takes it as a personal affront, I imagine," said Parker.

"I must remember that then if he ever has to perform on me." Manners chuckled.

Parker cleared his throat and called, "Before you all go, gentlemen, is there anything anyone could add to what has already been said? I might have to speak to some of you again of course, but now would be a good chance, if you can think of anything that might be relevant?"

There was a general muttering and shaking of heads. Parker looked at Carter and Walters. "If you two would just hang on for a moment."

They both sat back down and looked at him expectantly. When the last of the medical crew had left the room, he sat down and said, "Walters, can you add anything to the description you gave just now?"

"Well yes, Sir. I have been thinking about it, and there was one thing about his eyes that was bothering me and now I think I know what it was. Apart from them being probably the bluest blue that I have ever seen, the area around them looked a little odd; the look, I think now, of someone who is not wearing spectacles but usually does. And he had a slightly unusual gait, not a limp, exactly, but perhaps favouring one leg, or hip maybe."

"Thank you, Constable, that was very observant of you. Anything else?"

"No, Sir, he seemed very pleasant in his general demeanour and there was nothing about him to arouse any suspicion that he was anything other than what he purported to be."

"And what about his hair, then? What made you think it was dyed?"

"Oh, I'm pretty sure it was. My father-in-law dyes his, although everyone knows better than to mention it, and Mr. Sinclair's, or whoever he was, had the same look. And probably less expertly applied than my father-in-law's."

"So, you think there was probably some attempt at disguising his appearance, then?"

"I wouldn't have thought that was necessarily so, no. It is not unusual for men who are turning, or have turned, grey to try and hide the fact. Of course, with hindsight..."

"Quite so. Well, the sixty-four-dollar question is – would you recognise him again?"

"I can't honestly say that I would, Sir, apart from those eyes, which were most unusual, and the hair, there was little else that was remarkable. His nose and mouth were covered with the face mask of course. And oh yes, he was clean shaven, well as far as I could see he was. He may well have had a moustache or even some sort of small beard, like a Van Dyke or a Goatee perhaps; all I can say is that there was no hair visible at the sides of his mask, as there is with Mr. McGrath for example."

"Thank you. Now, Carter, is there anything that you can add? Was there anything unusual about any of the staff that entered the room that day during your shift?"

"Nothing of any relevance, Sir, that I can put a finger on.

There was, of course, the regular nursing staff and there was plenty of them but they invariably all closed the door behind then so I couldn't vouch for what went on. Other than the nurses and HCAs, er, that's 'Health Care Assistants', I'm told, there were the essential auxiliaries, like the cleaner." He consulted his notebook. "She went in at nine-oh-five and I was able to watch her because she left the door open. She mopped the floor and did a quick, perfunctory flip around with a damp cloth. There was the drinks trolley chap, of course, at about ten a.m. and again at just after three p.m. He just poked his head around the door, though, and Denton refused a drink on both occasions. An Asian girl went in, again with a trolley, at about," he consulted his notebook again, "eleven-fifteen and took a fresh jug of iced water and a glass to replace those already there."

"Two physiotherapists," again a look at his notebook, "Becky and Della. They spent about twenty-five minutes with him. They helped him out of bed and tried to get him to walk a few steps. They were lovely girls and patient to the extreme, but he was Bolshy and didn't want to do anything other than apparently to lie on his bed and whinge. A phlebotomist went in at nearly four p.m. to collect some more blood samples, and that was it, Sir."

"Right, thank you. I am sorry that you had to be called back here so soon after the end of your shift, I think you should log this as overtime and if your Inspector queries it, tell him to call me."

"Oh, well, thank you, Sir, my boss is usually pretty good about these things but I'm sure he will appreciate your endorsement."

Parker looked at Walters. "I believe you are on shift now, is that right?"

Walters agreed and Parker said, "Well, I want you back outside that door pronto. You will lock it and take personal possession of the key. That room is totally out of bounds to *anyone* until the forensics team arrive and I will arrange for them to come as soon as I get back to the station. Sergeant Manners will contact you and let you know the name of the SOCO as soon as we know it. Any questions?"

"No, Sir, I'll get straight back there now."

"Good man. Off you go then and don't hang about."

Parker turned to Manners. "Time to head back to the ranch, Dave. We have much to consider."

Nineteen

He drove slowly along Hadley Court Road with his front window lowered. The first house on the right past the bungalows looked scruffy and unkempt in sharp contrast with its neighbours; the front garden was overgrown with weeds and unmown grass and the paint was peeling off the front door and window frames. The paving slabs forming the path were cracked and weeds were growing through them. An old black BSA motorcycle stood on the path, tilted onto its prop stand and a patch of dirty engine oil stained the paving slabs beneath it. He took a series of photographs of the bike through the open window as he passed, being careful to keep his phone as unobtrusive as possible.

He noted that the bungalows were odd numbered, starting at one, and the one immediately next to this house was seven, the adjoining one was eleven so it was reasonable to assume that this was number nine although there was no number visible.

He drove on and at the end of the road he passed Hadley Court, a seventeenth-century manor House built for Sir James Hadley a local Squire and landowner. It had been requisitioned during the Second World War for use by the American Army, with the officers being quartered in the main building and a large number of troops housed in temporary huts erected in the grounds attached to the house. After the war it became a girls' school for a while and then a highly regarded restaurant. A few years ago, it had been converted into its current use as a retirement home.

When he got home, he booted up his laptop and spent nearly

an hour trying to identify the bike's model and age. From its registration number he was able to narrow its age down to 1958-60 with a reasonable degree of confidence. After comparing the pictures he had taken with models advertised for sale, mostly on Ebay, he was pretty sure that it was a 250cc model C15. Close enough. Prices varied, ranging from a few hundred up to many thousand for classics in superb condition. The machine that he had just seen looked to be in a very poor state; the saddle was ripped, the footrest rubbers were almost worn away and the oil stains on the path were a good indication of poor maintenance. It looked as if it hadn't been cleaned for years and most of the chrome work was rusted. Probably four or five hundred pounds at best.

He drove back to Hadley Court Road but parked just around the corner out of sight, then walked up to number nine. He stood on the path for a while and made a show of looking at the bike; he walked around it, poked a gloved finger into the split on the saddle covering then stooped down to examine the front forks. He was looking for a twitch of the grubby curtains but there was no sign of life, so he walked up to the front door and pressed the bell push with the knuckle of his middle finger.

There was no sound of a bell, so he pulled a coin from his pocket and used it to knock on the peeling paintwork of the door. Nothing. He rapped again, harder, and after a while the door was opened to reveal a tall, scruffy young man, probably in his mid-twenties, with long hair hanging round his face and reaching to just below his shoulders. He wore torn jeans and a grey T-Shirt with some illegible slogan printed across the front, and was barefooted. His eyes were bloodshot, and he squinted into the light. "What do you want?"

"Good afternoon, Sir, do you by any chance own this

machine?" He indicated the bike.

"What's that got to do with you?"

"Well, I am a bit of a Beesa buff, and I've been looking for a C15 that I could 'do up' for some time. So, I wondered if the owner of this one would be prepared to sell it. Are you the owner, Sir?"

"Well, yeah, I am but it ain't for sale."

"You haven't heard my offer yet." He saw a glint of greed in Peters' eyes.

"So, what are you offering then?"

"Well, as you obviously know it's not in the best condition, but as I would be restoring it, I would think about four hundred pounds would be a reasonable price."

"No way! It's worth far more than that."

"Perhaps I could go up to five then. But would you start it for me? I'd like to hear it."

"It starts dead easy and it's a good little runner."

"So would you start her up then?"

"Wait a minute." He closed the door, then reappeared with his feet stuffed into a pair of old trainers. He straddled the bike and eased it off the prop stand, opened the petrol tap and pumped the carburettor a couple of times then kicked the starter. On the third kick it roared into life, a cloud of oily smoke belching from the exhaust. He let it idle for a while then revved it a few times before allowing it to die. "Well?"

"Tappets sound a bit noisy and it's obviously burning a bit of oil, but I suppose that's fixable. You've got the V5 for it, of course?"

"V5? What's that?"

"The Vehicle Registration Certificate."

"Of course."

"And it's in your name?"

"Naturally."

"Have you registered it as 'historic'?"

"Why would I want to do that?"

"Because," he explained patiently, "a vehicle that is over forty years old can be registered as 'historic' and then it is exempt from Tax or MOT testing."

"Christ! I didn't know that!"

"Doesn't matter, I can do that easily enough. Try the lights now, please."

Peters switched on the headlights, dipped them then pressed the rear brake pedal. "Satisfied?"

"OK, shall we say five hundred then?"

Peters was wondering just how far he could push this sucker. He seemed to know what he was on about, but he had already offered far more than it was worth. He hadn't thought about selling it until this old guy came along and he didn't want to lose a chance like this. He knew he could pick up another bike from either of the two garages where the owners relied on him for their drug fixes, and a couple of days or maybe a week without a bike would be no real hardship. If he pushed too much the old guy was likely to just go away, and then he would have lost any bargaining power if he had to call him back. He did seem keen though. Perhaps one more shot. "Six and you've got yourself a bargain."

"No, I rather think not. You know as well as I do that five hundred is more than it's worth. So, it's five or nothing. And cash, of course. And include your crash helmet."

"Why would you want that?"

"Because I don't have mine down here and yours would do me until I can buy a new one."

"OK, then. Five hundred it is. How do we do this?"

"Do you know the new development on the site of the old allotments just on the left past the Duke's Head pub?"

"I know where it is but I ain't never been there why?"

"All the roads there are named after trees. Hawthorne Road is the main road into it, and Elder Close is a cul-de-sac and the last turning on the right. Not all the houses there have been occupied yet but mine is at the far end. Number seventeen. Bring the bike there tomorrow at five o'clock and don't forget the V5. That will give me time to get the money from the bank and I will give it to you, in cash, and we're done. OK?"

"OK, but how do I get back here then?"

"I'll run you back in my car."

"Right, but I don't even know your name, do I?"

"No, you don't," he said as he turned and walked back to where his car was parked around the corner.

Twenty

Elder Close had been well chosen. It was at the end of the new development and the last of the roads to be surfaced. Only four of the bungalows had so far been sold and they were at the entrance to the Close, number seventeen was semi-detached and at the far end. The rear of it backed onto a field and was not overlooked except for a small dairy herd of about two dozen Friesian cattle and an occasional tractor, neither of which showed any apparent interest whatsoever in the bungalows in Elder Close. The fronts had been landscaped with paved drives and turf but the interior decorating had yet to be completed. Ideal for what he had in mind. He drove to Elder Close, but parked about halfway along, outside another unoccupied bungalow. Both number plates had been smeared with mud but did not look too out of place as the rest of the car was pretty dirty – typical of a vehicle being used daily in a new rural development.

He checked his pockets carefully to be sure that he had all he needed, then walked to number seventeen. It was still ten minutes short of five o'clock, so he went round to the rear and leant against the back wall. The cattle were in a group at the far side of the field, doubtlessly waiting for the gate to be opened so that they could take the few minutes' walk to the milking parlour, to their own familiar stalls and the relief that the twice daily milking routine afforded them. They were Friesians he knew, or should they be called Holsteins? Either would be correct, but neither would worry them. As long as they had grass to chew and were milked on time their lives were contented and uncomplicated.

Until they could no longer produce a calf each year of course, and then... The sound of an approaching motorbike interrupted his thoughts. He took a pair of clear plastic gloves from his pocket and put them on then stepped around the side of the bungalow and waved to the rider. He indicated to him that he should come up the drive, then pointed round to the back. Peters stopped just short of the back, put his feet down and let the engine drop to an idle.

"Just bring it round the corner please and pull it onto its main stand."

Peters did as he was asked, then shut the engine down. He looked expectantly at his potential buyer and said, "Everything alright, then?"

"Oh, yes. Did you bring the V5?"

"Of course."

"May I just see it then, please?"

Peters reached inside his dirty leather jacket and drew out the V5 certificate in an old envelope. The 'buyer' glanced at it. "You are Cecil John Peters?"

"That's what it says."

"Yes, I *can* read, but is that you?"

Peters gave an exasperated sigh and said, "Yeah, that's me."

"Fine. Can I just see your helmet, please?"

Peters had already undone his chin strap, so he pulled the helmet off, and shook his head letting his pig-tail fall down his back then passed the helmet over to this pernickety old fool.

"That's good, so here's your money, five hundred pounds as agreed right?" He started to draw a thick white envelope from his pocket, then looked down at the front of the engine. "Hey, wait a minute, what the hell is *this*?"

"What's what?"

"*This!*"

Peters was still straddling the bike, so he kept his hold on the handlebar with his right hand and leant down to see what the man was pointing at. As his head came level with the petrol tank the helmet came down onto his head with all the force that the man could summon. His face was already turning in to face the engine so the blow caught him on the side of his head just above, and behind, his ear. He experienced a blinding pain for the split second before everything went black and the breath exploded from his lungs in an involuntary gasp. He collapsed down against the side of the bike, his head hitting the ground near the front wheel, his right arm slid across the top of the tank and fell loosely beside his body, but his right leg remained halfway across the saddle.

His attacker reached down and pushed the end of Peters' ponytail between the spokes of the front wheel, then, pulling the bike back on its stand to raise the wheel clear if the ground, he spun it slowly so that it dragged Peters' head hard against the front forks. He reached into his pocket and withdrew a packet of assorted plastic cable ties, the top of which he had already slit open. He selected three of the longest and connected them together, the tongue of one slipping into the square hole of the next. He bent down and loosened the top of Peters' leather jacket, then passed the cable ties around his neck. The length was about right, with perhaps a couple of inches to spare. He pushed the tongue through the square hole and pulled it gently, hearing the gentle click, click, click as the ratchet-like protrusion of the cable tie caught against the grooves. When it was nearly tight, he felt around it and under the chin then, satisfied with its position, he jerked it as hard as he could. He heard four or five more clicks as the plastic bit into the throat and neck, almost disappearing under the flesh. He gave the end of the cable tie another hard tug, but it was already as tight as it was ever going to be.

He felt for a pulse under Peters' ear but could feel nothing. He was by no means an expert at feeling pulses, so he tried again. Peters' face was already turning blue, and the flesh was swelling over the cable ties and, as far as he could tell, there was no pulse. He pulled the collar of the leather jacket back up hiding the ties, then retrieved the V5 in its envelope from where it had fallen and looked around.

Satisfied, he peered carefully around the corner of the bungalow and, seeing the cul-de-sac completely deserted, walked back to his car and drove away to the local garage and its car wash, confident that he had not been seen.

He had no idea when Peters' body might be discovered; could be within an hour or so but that seemed unlikely, could be a day or two, perhaps even a week. The likeliest scenario, he supposed, would be a decorator coming to decorate the bungalow but, if many of the other buildings were also unfinished, number seventeen could be way down the list, so there was no telling when that might be. Not that it mattered much, but he rather hoped it would be before the refuse bins in Preston Way were emptied.

It was much later, and quite dark, when he drove back along a deserted Preston Way and found that, as Harry Denton had predicted and he had confirmed the previous night, the old Ford van parked outside number thirty-four was unlocked but the rear doors were. He noticed that there was a red Toyota parked a few yards behind it but paid it no attention. The refuse bins were left at the front of the house. "Lazy sod," he thought, "but convenient!"

Twenty-One

Chief Inspector Parker was about to head to the incident room for his morning's briefing when his phone rang. "Good morning Chief Inspector, this is Bob McGrath from Elmington General."

"Oh, good morning, Bob. Does this mean you have some news for me?"

"Indeed, I have. We have received the Postmortem report from Doctor Jessop, our pathologist, and Mr. Connaught thought you might like to hear the gist of it before we got a copy to you. We wouldn't email it of course, for privacy reasons, so we would ask you to arrange to collect from here, but we think it is interesting enough to warrant a little short cutting."

"Oh, this sounds a little ominous. Could you perhaps hang on a minute while I find Dave Manners, I'd like him to hear this, if you don't mind?"

"Not at all, Chief Inspector."

"Reg, please."

"OK, Reg, by all means get Dave in."

Parker opened his door and saw Manners just leaving, on his way to the incident room. "Dave, in here please."

As Manners entered the room, Parker indicated a chair and switched his phone to speaker. "OK, Bob, Dave is here now and I've switched my phone to speaker – so, shoot, we're all ears."

"Morning, Dave. I was just telling Chief Inspector, er, Reg, that we have the Postmortem report from Doctor Jessop and it makes interesting reading. Jon Reynolds was absolutely right, of course, as we had no doubt he would be, cause of death was indeed a massive cardiac arrest, or heart attack to you. But it was the *cause* of the arrest that is of interest. It was caused by a venous embolism, and, in turn, *its* cause was undoubtedly iatrogenic."

"Whoa, there Robert," interjected Dave, "could we have that in English please? Remember we are just simple Coppers, here."

"Sorry, Dave, I'm not trying to show off, but I thought it better to give you Doctor Jessop's words first, then explain any of it in plain English as necessary."

"Thanks," said Parker, "can we start with the Venus bit, then, please?"

"Venous," corrected McGrath, "venous embolism. An embolism is a blockage of an artery or vein, usually by an air bubble, so a venous embolism simply means a blockage of a vein. It's the sort of thing that divers are susceptible to if they surface too quickly from any depth, although in their case it would likely be nitrogen bubbles that form. In Mr. Denton's case it was almost certainly just plain old air, or at least, it was as far as Ken Jessop could determine, and he's pretty sharp. So, there was a large bubble of air in his vein which worked its way into his heart and – Bingo! Cardiac arrest. And iatrogenic means that it was introduced by medical intervention. In a nutshell, gentlemen, someone injected a fairly large volume of air into Mr. Denton's vein. And, considering that he had a cannula conveniently stuck into said vein, it wouldn't have needed a medically trained genius to administer it."

There was silence while Parker and Manners absorbed this bombshell. "Are you still there?" asked McGrath.

"Oh, yes, Bob, we are just trying to digest this. So, tell me, how long would it be between injecting the air and, um, the er…?"

"Probably about five minutes or so, I would say, it was quite a large bubble according to Ken Jessop. They tend to dissipate fairly quickly but there was still enough in there for him to be sure of the facts."

"So that had to be our wannabe Mr. Sinclair then?" said Parker.

"I couldn't possibly say that, could I?" said Bob. "I am just a simple sawbones, not a simple copper, but if I was, I think that is probably the conclusion that I would come to."

"Christ!" said Parker. "Er, I mean, good Heavens! But tell me, Bob, just how much medical knowledge would someone need to do this? It all sounds highly technical to me. Are we looking for someone with medical training or would any old plumber's mate know enough to do it? I know that this simple Copper would never have dreamed of it, but then, perhaps I am too simple?"

"I don't think either of you two buggers are anywhere near as simple as you look, er, I mean, as you pretend to be. But I think that you would probably be better talking to Ken Jessop, really, I was asked only to give you the basic PM findings, but if you don't quote me, let me just say this – the Internet is a wondrous thing, but it contains a lot of information that is perhaps not always necessary or helpful to law abiding folk. And anyone who has spent any time in a hospital, and there are lamentably few that haven't, will be well aware of cannulas and intravenous drips, even if they don't know the names of them. And non-needled syringes can be bought almost anywhere – even garden centres, would you believe? They are apparently used for measuring concentrated weed killer or fertiliser, so maybe a gardener rather than your plumber's mate? Of course, it couldn't be done if the patient was resisting, but if the er, 'perpetrator' do you call them, found some way of making Denton *want,* or think he *needed* the injection, obviously not knowing it was going to be just air... it would not be too difficult. But, for pity's sake, don't even think of calling me as 'an expert witness' or my Lord and Master would not be amused, and a 'death by a thousand cuts' at his hands would not particularly amuse me either!

"There is one other thing perhaps you should know. The toxicology tests confirmed our suspicions that he was a fairly well-established 'user'. There was a large quantity of very low-grade heroin in his blood stream, so, considering he had been unable to access any since he had been under our care, he must have been quite heavily loaded when he came in. There were needle marks aplenty, but Ken tends to the view that he was more of a 'snorter' than an injector, at least in the more recent months, anyway."

Parker thanked McGrath, and he and Manners headed for the incident room.

Twenty-Two

"Gather round, everybody, and listen up," said Parker, "we have just had a report of the Postmerten findings on Harry Denton, and although I do not yet have a full copy, Mr. Connaught's Registrar, Bob McGrath, has given Sergeant Manners and I a comprehensive précis of it and managed to put most of the important bits into plain English for us.

"In a nutshell, this has now become a murder enquiry. Someone purporting to be a doctor, or a surgeon, to be precise, injected a large volume of air into the cannular attached to Harry Denton's arm and this apparently travelled along his vein and into his heart, causing a massive heart attack. We have some sort of description of the killer but not good enough to identify him positively. The motive could well be revenge, after all, we are pretty sure that he was involved, with two others, in a mugging which resulted in the death of an elderly lady and some injuries to her husband, but we will not make any pre-judgements." He drew attention to the board that had been created. At the centre were Richard and Mary Fleming with coloured lines leading from them to Denton and the four possible associates. "This, of course, needs to be updated. Denton is no longer just a suspect, but a victim as well. There is a lot of work to be done here but first, let's hear some reports of what you have so far. He looked at DC Watson. "Beryl, I believe you had the address for the Filipino nurse. Did you and Pete Lee see her and get a statement?"

"Yes, Guv. She remembers him well but was able to offer little more than Constable Walters gave us. She was intrigued by his eyes, though; she said that she had never seen eyes so blue. I thought that was due to the fact that there are probably very few blue-eyed people in the Philippines, but Pete pointed out that she has been resident in the UK for over seven years so has had plenty of chances of seeing some here. So perhaps we can assume that they were, if not unusual, then certainly striking. She also said that he 'spoke funny'. I asked if that meant he had a foreign accent, but she said, 'No, but not proper English, perhaps like an Irish or a Scotland person. And he called me Lassie.' She said that as he was leaving, she asked him to sign for some medication for one of her patients who was in pain, but he said that he could not stop as he had been paged to attend A&E urgently."

Parker said, "Thank you, that ties in with Walters' impression of a 'Scottish burr'. And we know that A&E knew nothing of him, so I have no doubt at all that he was as phoney as an honest politician. Anything to add to that, Pete?"

"Not really, Guv, I think Beryl has covered it well, and she did most of the chatting with her. I did ask her if she had worked at City Royal and she said that she had, but had not met the real Mr. Sinclair, as far as she was aware. And most of her work at the General had been in the maternity ward, though, so she would not be very familiar with the orthopaedic doctors anyway."

"Maternity ward? Is she a midwife, then?"

"No, Sir," interrupted Beryl, "I wondered the same thing, that it would be odd for a midwife to be deployed onto a surgical ward, but apparently midwifery is not an essential prerequisite for the maternity suite, and a lot of general nurses are employed there all the time."

"Oooh, 'essential prerequisite', what have you been reading,

Beryl dear?!" smirked 'Ronnie' Corbett.

"Corbett!" snapped Parker. "Cut it out! This is a murder enquiry briefing, not the Edinburgh Fringe!"

"Sorry, Guv."

Parker looked around, but there were no other comments. "Dave?"

"Yes, Guv. I think this may not be quite so clear cut as it may appear. At first sight, yes, the motive would certainly seem to be revenge as you suggested, and, of course, that would make Richard Fleming the top suspect. After all he and his wife were mugged, almost certainly by Denton and his mates, and we know that, sadly, his wife subsequently died from the injuries that she sustained in that attack. But Pete and I both think that it is unlikely to be him. He is seventy-eight years old, is registered as disabled and walks only with the aid of a stick, the stick incidentally that was responsible for Denton being in the general in the first place. He is not exactly frail, but certainly his capabilities would be limited. We have no doubt that he is an intelligent man and would, if he were younger and fitter, be a natural candidate for prime suspect. I would like to visit him again, with Pete, and give him the news of Denton's death and see how he reacts. I am not saying that he couldn't possibly have done this, I'm just saying that it seems improbable, and we should keep an open mind.

"I think we should also consider the possibility of a drugs connection too. Bob McGrath just told us that the Postmortem found evidence of heroin in Denton's blood and he had a screw of heroin in his pocket when he was admitted to the general, and his demeanour since then could well suggest some withdrawal symptoms. And Jacques, who is a strong suspect as one of Denton's accomplices," he tapped the display board, "has convictions for possessing class-A drugs with intent to supply. I would like to suggest, Guv, that when we pick them up, we are armed with search warrants for all these premises."

"That's good thinking, Dave, you and Pete have seen Richard Fleming so you would be the best judges of his mobility, etc., but just be aware that he *could* be playing up the disability card a bit. As far as the search warrants are concerned, we may well have a problem convincing the Magistrate to sign one for Miller, given his ethnic origin and the witness's statements, so we'll hold back on his until we've interviewed him, but we will certainly get one for Jacques and Peters."

***

He turned back to the display board and said, "Beryl, can you bring us up to date on these four, please?"

"Yes, Guv, I think we now have enough to identify them. As I said before, we have a definite address for Colin Jacques, and I have narrowed down 'Amos' Miller. As I suspected, Amos is not his real name, but I found an A.M. Miller who turns out to be an Afro-Caribbean whose name is Albert Mostyn – so I think that is a pretty good bet for 'Amos'. Denton's brother Frank was easy, and I would suggest that a simple visit to him should put him either in the clear or in the frame. The former, I suspect."

"Thank you, Beryl, go on."

"Zack Peters. Again, not his real name. There are four 'Peters' on the Electoral Register; two of the addresses have only a married couple registered, and they are both way too old to be considered. Of the other two, one is a Barrister with his wife with a five-year-old daughter, and while I would hesitate to suggest that a barrister could be above suspicion, this one is in his fifties so can safely be discounted, I'm afraid. That leaves the other address which has a twenty-five-year-old named Cecil; obviously not a 'cool' enough name for someone who has previous for possession of a class-A drug with intent to supply'. And when his property was searched, a rather pathetic attempt at growing marijuana was found in his attic, so I think we can be pretty confident that Cecil is our lad."

"That is excellent, Beryl. I think Miller may be a red herring, as neither of our witnesses mentioned anyone of Afro-Caribbean appearance, but it was late enough for the light to be unhelpful at best. So, we keep him in."

"OK, Guv."

"I want a synchronised pick-up at six a.m. tomorrow. Sergeant Manners will allocate the three teams for the pick-ups and dedicate a radio channel, and I want all three kept incommunicado until we have spoken to Denton's brother. I will be co-ordinator for the pick-ups. To save time, Dave Manners will arrange for Frank Denton to be interviewed tomorrow morning, at his home, unless he proves to be uncooperative, of course, in which case he will be brought in with the other suspects. And it occurs to me, Dave, that as Jacques seems rather large and is likely to be uncooperative, or violent, even, you may wish to collect him yourself, possibly with the 'bungalow' for company, of course."

There were barely concealed chuckles and giggles, then, as Parker turned to leave the room, he snapped, "Corbett! My office. Now!"

Lee gave Dave a hard look and said, "Bungalow? Our nice Mr. Fleming has got a lot to answer for."

"Oh, take no notice of 'Nosy', Pete, that's just his not very subtle way of telling us that he knows everything that goes on!"

Twenty-Three

Corbett tapped on Parker's door. "Come in. Shut the door." He stood in front of Parker's desk. "Yes, Guv?"

"Sir!"

"Sorry, yes, Sir."

"Corbett. I have told you before and I will tell you just this once more that I am not prepared to tolerate many more of your inane, snide remarks to D.C. Watson. She is a damn fine officer and I find your attitude towards her offensive in the extreme."

"It was just a little banter, Sir."

"Balls! If you consider that 'banter', I suggest you try it on Pete Lee and see if you find his reaction quite so amusing."

"I'm sorry, Sir."

"And you need to be. I shall enter this on your record as a formal warning, and if there is any more of it you will be off my team before your feet can touch the ground. Got it?"

"Yes, Sir, and I will apologise to Beryl, er, D.C. Watson straight away." A very contrite 'Ronnie' Corbett left the office and went over to Beryl Watson to offer his apologies just as Dave Manners was calling for attention. "Listen up, everybody. Ronnie, I want you to check on Frank Denton, now, just to see if he will be around tomorrow morning. Don't give any indication of who you are and why you want to know. Now, the teams for the morning will be…" He consulted a paper in his hand and said, "The three teams for the pick-up will be; myself, Lee and Patel will collect Jacques; Robertson, Mohammed and Phillips will collect Miller and White, Watson and Pearson will get Peters. The first two names I mentioned of each team will do the actual collecting, so that's myself and Pete, Robby and Ahmed, and Chalky with Beryl. The third man will stand by at the rear of the premises in case anyone does a runner and will also remain behind with the search warrant, but will wait for our uniformed brethren to back up the search.

"Each car will park up around the nearest corner, out of sight of the premises by ten minutes to six and establish the communications link. Then wait for Chief Inspector Parker's orders. On his word you will drive up to the premises and confirm that you, and your third man, are in position. On Mr. Parker's command, and, knowing him, that will be six a.m. on the dot, you will knock the doors. If there is no response but you *know* that someone is in there, you will force an entry as necessary without delay; we don't want any evidence disappearing down the loo, do we? If the place genuinely appears to be empty, which is highly unlikely, you will report to Chief Inspector Parker for further instructions. If any of you are unsure of the addresses there is a large-scale map on the incident board, so familiarise yourselves with it this evening – I don't want any of you getting lost on your way there! All three suspects are to be brought back here without delay and they will be held in separate interview rooms, which will be allocated by the Custody Sergeant. On no account are they to communicate with anyone, although it would do no harm if they see each other. Any questions?"

"Yes, Sarg." Corbett was just replacing his phone. "Frank Denton works for a travel agency and at the moment is actually on a familiarisation cruise around the Eastern Med. It seems they do that during the quiet times so that they can advise potential customers from a first-hand perspective. At the moment he is probably somewhere near Gib on his way back. So, he wouldn't have been in the country when the attack took place."

"Thanks, Ronnie. We can write him off then. Has anyone anything else to offer or query? No? OK, that's it, then."

Twenty-Four

At nine minutes to six on Sunday morning, Parker's radio crackled into life. "Papa Control from Papa One. In position. Over."

"Papa One, Roger. Standby, out."

"Papa Control from Papa Three. In position. Over."

"Papa Three, Roger. Standby, out."

"Papa Control from Papa Two. In position. Over."

"Papa Two, Roger. Standby, out."

Five minutes passed, then, "Papas One, Two and Three. Move to premises and report when ready."

All three cars moved into position outside their respective premises and the 'third man' went around the back to cover the rear entrances. They all reported to Parker and at exactly six o'clock he gave the order for them to proceed.

***

Robertson and Mohammed banged on Miller's door and, after a few moments the door opened to reveal 'Amos' Miller enveloped in a huge, multi-coloured Kaftan. "Good morning, Sir, are you Albert Mostyn Miller?"

"Long time since I been call dat but yus, I am, and who be you?"

They both showed their warrant cards and Robertson said, "I wonder if we might come in for a moment, Sir? We have a few questions that you may be able to help us with."

Miller looked puzzled but opened the door for them. "What's de problem, den?"

"We would like you to accompany us to the station if you would, Sir, it shouldn't take too long."

"Why don't you ask me here?"

"We would prefer to do it at the station, Sir."

"I ain't done nothin' wrong, you know."

"I'm sure that's right, Sir, but we just need to eliminate you from our enquiries."

"Enquiries about what?"

"We'll explain all that at the station, Sir."

"You don't be arresting me den?"

"We would much rather you accompany us of your own free will."

"OK, den, but I gonna have to put some proper clothes on."

"Of course, Sir, Ahmed, would you mind?" Mohammed nodded and went with Miller while he changed into a pair of old jeans and a T-shirt, then with him into the back of the car. Robby called Pat Phillips, and told him to remain at the premises until they had interviewed Miller and decided whether to apply for a search warrant or not. They then returned to the station.

***

'Chalky' White and Beryl Watson got no response to their hammering on Peters' door and they could see no of sign of movement in the house. Chalky called Phil Pearson who was watching the rear and he confirmed that there was no sign of any activity there either. "Can't see upstairs, of course, but it's all pretty deserted down here."

White radioed Parker, "White here, Guv. We are at Hadley Court Road, but the place appears to be empty, at least of people. There is a large oil stain on the front path which looks as if a motor-bike is usually parked there but there is no sign of it. It may be a bit early for door-to-door stuff yet, Guv, so what would you like us to do? It doesn't look as though it would be too difficult to force an entry, though I think the rear would be the best bet."

"No, don't do that yet. Find somewhere to park up where you can keep the house under observation in case he turns up. Then start door-to-door enquiries at about seven, or earlier if you see any of the good Burghers of Hadley Court Road up and about before then. If he has left, find out when and, if possible, where, etc. Keep me informed."

***

As Sunni Patel left the car to take up his post at the rear of Jacques' house, Manners warned him, "Keep on your toes, Sunni, there is every chance that this bugger will try and make a run for it and if he does, you stop him. We wouldn't want to lose him, would we?"

"Of course, Sarg, and he would be one very lucky bugger indeed to get passed Sunni the Superman!"

"Well, just make sure you don't have to eat those words. Because if he does run out the back it will probably mean that he has given little Peter here the slip, and I don't know many that could do that."

"Oh, Golly Gosh, Sergeant, Sir, in that case, I shall put my underpants on over my tights and prepare to apprehend this beast with all due diligence!"

"Yes, well get round the back quick, then, you daft bugger!"

On Parker's 'go', he and Pete ran up to the front door and knocked long and loud. They were aware of some movement in the house, so Manners shouted through the letterbox, "Police. Open up. Now. Or we'll force an entry. Your choice. Mr. Jacques."

Jacques opened the door slightly and, as he did so, Lee put his shoulder against it forcing it wide open and sending Jacques staggering backwards, struggling to keep his balance. "Hey, what the Hell's all this?"

Manners quickly followed Lee through the door. "Good morning, Sir, are you Colin Frederick Jacques?"

"Who the hell are you and who is this great gorilla? You've got no right busting in here like this..."

Manners and Lee both produced their warrant cards and held them up in his face. "I am Detective Sergeant Manners, and my colleague is Detective Constable Lee who has a particular aversion to being called rude names, so I suggest you watch your tongue rather carefully. We would like you to accompany us to the station to answer a few questions, if you would be so kind."

"Balls! I ain't going nowhere with you."

"Oh, I'm afraid you are. It's just that it would be a little easier if you came willingly."

"I said no. Don't you understand that?"

"In that case, Colin Frederick Jacques, I am arresting you on suspicion of assault causing actual bodily harm. You do not have to say anything, but it may harm your defence if..."

Jacques looked towards the front door, but it was blocked by Manners. He panicked, spun on his heel and made a dash for the kitchen door at the end of the hall. Pete pushed past Dave and in three strides had caught Jacques just as he fumbled with the doorknob. He wrapped a hand the size of a small shovel around his throat, pulled him backwards and slammed his back against the wall with enough force to rattle the doors, "Now, that was not very polite, was it? Running off when the Sergeant was talking to you."

"...Anything you do say may be given in evidence," continued Manners as though there had been no interruption. "Do you understand?"

"I can't bleedin' breathe," gasped Jacques. He was gurgling and clawing ineffectually at Lee's hand which was still clamped around his throat.

Lee eased him away from the wall, then thumped him back again. "DO," thump, "YOU," thump, "UNDER," thump, "STAND?" Thump.

"Yes."

"Yes, what?"

"Yes, I understand. And leggo my bleedin' throat."

"Turn round." Lee pulled him away from the wall then slid his left hand behind Jacques' back, grabbed his left shoulder and spun him round so that he was facing the wall, he pressed him hard into it and held him there with his left forearm across his back.

"Put your hands behind your back, please."

Jacques was struggling. Manners said, "Better do as he asks, Mr. Jacques, the last chap that he had to assist with that ended up with two dislocated shoulders, poor thing."

Jacques grunted and swiftly put his hands behind him, and Lee unhooked his handcuffs from his belt and snapped them on. He pulled him away from the wall and towards the front door. "Right, off we jolly well go," he said brightly. "That wasn't too hard, now, was it?"

Jacques spat a string of invectives at him. "Oh, language Colin! Obviously you've been reading 'How to Win Friends and Influence People' haven't you?"

As Pete put Jacques into the back of their car, Manners called Patel back and gave him the search warrant. "Sunni, I want you to stay here. No one to enter, of course. Mr. Parker has already arranged for a couple of uniforms to assist with the search of the premises, and I want a thorough search, every nook and cranny, any outbuildings and the garage. I would be very surprised if you don't find plenty of evidence of drug activity, but don't limit the search to that. OK?"

"Got it, Sarge. Can I start looking round before the boys in blue get here?"

"Most certainly not! You never conduct a search, of property or people, single-handed. That leaves you wide open to claims that you planted evidence, etc., so that is a very definite no, no."

"Thanks, Sarge. In that case I will await with delighted anticipation the arrival of our uniformed comrades."

"Oh, get on, you flannelling Asian person, you!"

"Cor, Sergeant, Sir, is that a racist remark, do you think?"

"Certainly not."

"Oh, good. Then I shall assume a position of authority at the door of this humble abode and await re-enforcements."

"Yes," thought Manners, "and you are nothing like the daft bugger you pretend to be, Sunni boy!"

***

Parker had returned to his office and was catching up on the large number of emails that had 'snuck in on him' as he would put it when his phone rang. "Chief Inspector Parker."

"Guv? Chalky White here. Had a bit of luck in Hadley Court Road. We haven't started the door-to-door stuff yet, but one of the neighbours who lives opposite number nine, a delightful old chap called Henry Winston, came out about six-thirty, with his dog, on his way to collect his morning paper. He says that he heard Peters' bike leave here Friday afternoon, probably just before five, he thinks, and, to the best of his knowledge, it hasn't been back since. I asked if he saw him leave but he said no, he just heard the bike. When I asked him if he was sure it was Peters, he said no, he wasn't! I was restraining myself from throttling him when he grinned and said, he wasn't sure that it was Peters, but he *was* sure that it was his bike. He said the exhaust was particularly noisy, there was some chain rattle and the tappets needed adjusting. He also said that he had ridden motor bikes himself for nearly fifty years until Anno Domino forced him to hang up his helmet, so I'm inclined to believe him.

"He also intimated that we would be wasting our time calling on any others along here because, as he put it, they are all past their sell-by dates, and most of them are deaf as posts! An exaggeration, I'm sure, and we'll do the door-to-door anyway, of course.

"He said that Peters lives there by himself; his mother died some six years or so ago and left the house to him. She was, he said, a lovely lady and totally different from her wastrel son for whom, I gather, the good Mr. Winston had precious little time."

"Thank you, Chalky, that's excellent. I will get Billings, to call there as soon as they can and I'll get a search team there, then you can start a search of the premises, and I want a thorough job of it, right? Keep the door-to-door going, though, and let me know if there is anything to add." Billings & Sons were a local Locksmiths who were usually first choice for the police to use and were used to being called out at all hours. John Billings, the owner, arrived at Hadley Court Road about half an hour after Parker's call. He chose the back door rather than the front, and Chalky White was impressed to see that he had it open within three minutes.

Twenty-Five

Parker and Manners entered interview room one where Miller sat at a small table and a uniformed constable stood just inside the door. They indicated to the escort that he should leave, and then took their seats opposite Miller. Manners switched on the recorder and, when its starting tone stopped, announced, "The time is nine-fifty-eight a.m.. I am Detective Sergeant David Manners, also present is Detective Chief Inspector Reginald Parker and Mr. Albert Mostyn Miller. Mr. Miller, this interview is being recorded."

Parker said, "Mr. Miller, you are here voluntarily to answer some questions about an incident that took place in Harpers Lane on Tuesday, the fifteenth of this month, and we thank you for your assistance. However, I must caution you that you do not have to say anything. But it may harm your defence if you do not mention when questioned something which you later rely on in court. Anything you do say may be given in evidence."

"But I'm not under arrest, though, am I? Do I need a solicitor?"

"No, Mr. Miller, you are not under arrest. If you would like a solicitor to be present, we can, of course, arrange that for you, but at the moment we wish only to eliminate you from our enquiries. Do you wish us to suspend this interview and arrange for a solicitor to attend?"

"No, dat'll be alright den. But if I tink you are bullying me I can ask for one, right?"

Manners said, "Absolutely, Sir, but I can assure you that we have no intention of bullying you."

"OK, den, ask what you like."

"Thank you, Mr. Miller," said Parker. "May we firstly clear up the matter of your identity? You are Albert Mostyn Miller but are usually known as Amos, is that right?"

"Yessir, I was christened Albert Mostyn but only my Mamma ever call me Alby, ever one else call me Amos cos I like dat better."

"That's fine, thank you. May we call you Amos?"

"Yessir."

"Good, now, Amos, would you tell us please where you were on Tuesday the fifteenth of this month between the hours of eight and ten pm?"

"Why you wanna know dat?"

"Just answer the question, please."

"OK. So on Tuesdays I play arrers for de Dirty Duck A-team and on the fifteenth, um, yes we be home den, so I be at the Dirty Duck all evening."

"Arrers? The Dirty Duck?"

Manners interjected, "By 'arrows', do you mean darts? And do I take it that the Dirty Duck is the local term for the Black Swan Inn?"

"Yessir, of course. I play darts at de Dirty, er de Black Swan on Tuesdays Sir."

"And you were there on the fifteenth?"

"Oh, yessir."

"All evening? What time did you leave?"

"Well, Sir, I leave home at seven, so I be dere 'bout twenty past and we start de match at eight o'clock and we finish de game 'bout ten. Den we haves another pint 'praps and go home 'bout half past when dey shuts."

"And you did that on the Tuesday in question?"

"Oh, yessir, and we beat de Tree Lions somethin' cruel, too," he said proudly.

"Is there anyone who can vouch for you there, Amos?"

"All de team of course. And I see Jacko here when I come in, so him can tell you."

"Jacko?"

"Yessir, Colin Jacques, we call him Jacko, him on de team too."

"So, are you saying," asked Parker, "that Colin Jacques was playing darts with you at the Black Swan on Tuesday the fifteenth?"

"No, Sir, I ain't saying dat. Cos him don't play dat night. Him only reserve player and Jacko don't like dat. We all has to be reserve sometime don't we? But him get sulky, but him have to be dere, at least for de start, case someone don't come, but dat night we all come so him don't play. Him just have couple of drinks den him go home. Very sulky."

"So, what time would he have left then, would you say?"

"Oh, afore nine for sure. Him very sulky, don't know why, we all has to be reserve sometimes don't we?"

"And can anyone vouch for you after nine?"

"Sure. All de team. And dat nasty lil barman boy. Him new dere, but him 'member Amos for certain sure."

"And why would that be then?"

"Because him stupid! Him try to shortchange Amos and dat am a very stupid ting to do. Him try to give me change for ten but Amos give him twenty. And ever one see dat, so Amos tell him, 'You try cheat Amos, Boy and you likely get a set of arrers up yo jacksy'. Den de Landlord come over and him know Amos a good man and troofull, so him tell dis stupid boy to 'pologise to Amos and give de right money. So, I tink him remember Amos for sure, Sir."

"And who is the Captain of your team, Amos?"

"O, dat Willie Wonka."

Parker and Manners exchanged glances. "Who?"

"Willie Wonka. Of course, dat ain't him real name. Him really William Walton but we all calls him Willie Wonka cos Willie Walton sound like Willie Wonka an him like de chocolate bars so we..."

"Yes, yes, we get it. Do you have a phone number for him?"

"Course. Just in case we be sick or someting an' can't play, den we rings him up an' tells him."

"And what is his number, then?"

"I don't know. I got it at home, but Amos don't 'member all dem numbers. De landord of de Dirty Duck, him know for sure."

"Thank you, Amos. We will just check that out, and if he confirms your story then you will be free to go," said Parker giving a nod to Manners.

"Dat ain't no story, dat de troof man."

"Yes, of course, Amos, I didn't mean to imply that it wasn't."

For the benefit of the tape, Manners said, "Detective Sergeant Manners is leaving the room temporarily at ten-oh-eight." He left the room, closing the door behind him, acknowledged the constable who was waiting outside and returned to his desk, where he phoned the Black Swan. Luckily, the landlord answered and was able to give him Walton's phone number. It was a mobile number so Manners was able to call him straight away and was able to speak to him at his place of work. He confirmed almost exactly what Miller had told them and that it was indeed well after ten before they left the pub. Manners thanked him, rang off and returned to the interview room.

"Detective Sergeant Manners has re-entered the room at ten-twenty-four. Thank you, Mr. Miller, you have been most helpful. Mr. Walton has confirmed everything that you told us, so I don't think we need to detain you any longer. Chief Inspector?"

"Quite right, you are free to leave, Amos. Interview terminated at ten-twenty-six a.m." He turned off the recorder and removed the twin tapes; he and Manners both signed them and he slipped them into his pocket and all three left the room.

They watched Miller leave the building then returned to Parker's office. "Well, I've done some interviews in my time, Dave, but that's one for the memoires and no mistake!" They both chuckled. "I never really fancied him for that job, though, but we needed to be sure. And it sounded as if that new boy at the Dirty Duck had an object lesson in barmanship and who not to try to short-change, hmm?"

"Yes, Guv, our Amos may well be a bit of a rogue, but he's clean on this one and he's given us a helpful insight into any phony alibi that 'Jacko' might try on. And, speaking of 'Jacko', perhaps we should start to interview him? Is the Duty Solicitor here yet, do you know?"

"She is indeed," replied Parker with a grimace, "and it's Helen Greenway, Heaven help us!" He waved Dave towards the door. "Lead on, Macduff."

Twenty-Six

Parker and Manners entered interview room two and nodded an acknowledgement to Helen Greenway, the Duty Solicitor who was sitting next to Jacques. They dismissed the constable who was standing inside the door and sat at the table. Manners broke the seals on two new tapes, inserted them into the recorder and switched it on. "Before we start," said Greenway, "my client..." Parker held up his hand to silence her. "One moment, Madam, please wait until the recorder is running." The recorder emitted a single, long tone to indicate that it was in the 'record' mode, and Manners ran through the introductory routine of identifying those present. When he had finished, Parker nodded to Greenway. "You were saying?"

"I was about to say that my client wishes to lodge a complaint."

"Oh, yes?"

"He says that he was assaulted by one of your officers at his home when you arrested him this morning."

"That is absolute nonsense," said Manners, "we asked him if would come into the station to answer some questions, but he refused, and quite abusively I might say, so I arrested him on suspicion of assault causing actual bodily harm. Whilst I was cautioning him, he tried to run away, but Detective Constable Lee caught up with him and restrained him, using only the minimum force necessary to do that. I continued with the caution and your client was then handcuffed and brought in here."

"That is not how my client tells it, Sergeant."

"Then your client is fantasizing, Madam."

Parker broke in. "Your client, Madam, has been arrested on suspicion of assault as Sergeant Manners has already said, but there are other, more serious charges which he is likely to face. You should be aware that Mrs. Mary Fleming, the lady who was the victim of the assault for which Mr. Jacques is a suspect, has subsequently died from the injuries that she sustained during that attack."

Greenway frowned, obviously unaware of that development. "I would like a word alone with my client. And with you, Chief Inspector."

Parker nodded and said, "This interview is temporarily suspended at ten-fifty-two a.m." He indicated for Greenway to follow himself and Manners out of the room, then told the uniformed constable to resume his guard inside the room. Once in the corridor, he said, "Well?"

Greenway was fuming. "Why was I not informed of this before?"

"If you'd had the courtesy to call in my office when you arrived instead of steaming straight here as though you owned the place, I would naturally have updated you completely on the situation. You've been in this game long enough to know the routine, Madam, so please don't come the injured party act with me. Our interactions are expected to act both ways."

Greenway looked a bit mollified. "Oh, well, I'm sorry, then. Yes, of course I should have called on you, that is my normal practice, as you know. May I have a private word with my client now, please?"

"Of course, and please indicate to the constable when you are ready to resume."

As the door closed behind her, Parker said, "Not often we're able to surprise the White Witch, Dave!" They chatted together for a few minutes, then the constable opened the door and indicated that they should re-enter. They took their seats and Dave switched the recorder back on and made the usual announcements. Parker addressed himself to Jacques. "I will remind you, Mr. Jacques, that you are still under caution. Now, where were you on Tuesday the fifteenth of this month between the hours of eight p.m. and ten p.m.?"

Jacques looked at his solicitor, then at the floor and shook his head.

"Where were you, Mr. Jacques? I would like an answer."

No answer.

"We believe that, at that time, you were assaulting an elderly couple in Harpers Lane, Kings Dalton, together with two others, one of whom got a crack across his shin from the gentleman's walking stick for his trouble."

"No comment."

"We have two witnesses who can identify you. Was it you who grabbed Mrs. Fleming's handbag and punched her in the face? Did you strike Mr. Fleming and then kick him in the ribs as he lay on the ground trying to protect his wife?"

"It wasn't me. I wasn't there."

"Then where were you?"

"I was at the Black Swan pub, playing darts."

"No, I don't think you were."

"I was! Look, I saw Amos here when I came in and he can tell you. We've been playing at the Swan for years, him and me."

"So, what time did you leave the Black Swan that evening, then?"

"About when they shut, I think, gone ten anyway."

"You're lying."

"I ain't lying, I was there."

"Yes, I believe you were, but not until ten. You left well before nine, so you had ample time to join up with your mates, didn't you? And, of course, it would need three of you to take on an elderly lady and try to steal her handbag wouldn't it? Even though her husband was disabled and could walk only with the aid of a stick. Quite the macho trio."

"That ain't true. I didn't leave the pub 'til after ten I tell yer."

"We have several witnesses who will swear, on oath, that you left there before nine o'clock."

"Oh, Amos, was it? Well, you can't trust what he says, he was well pissed by then."

"Drunk, do you mean? While he was playing darts for the A-team? I think not. And we have statements from the team captain and also from the landlord, so think again."

Jacques looked at his solicitor, then, when she nodded, said, "No comment."

"No lies, you mean."

"No comment."

"Do you wish to tell me what really happened in Harpers Lane? Was it you who called for an Ambulance for Harry Denton?"

"No comment."

Manners interjected, "Do you know where Zack Peters is?"

"Zack? Why?"

"Where is he?"

"I dunno. I ain't seen him for a couple of weeks."

Parker cut in again. "You are lying again. You were with him and Harry Denton when you attacked that couple. You really ought to come clean about this you know, we have evidence enough to prove that you were there and with your record, now, what is it?" He referred to the papers he had in front of him. "Oh, yes, two counts of assault, three of breaking and entering and one of GBH, not to mention several for drug related offences, shall I go on? I am sure that your solicitor here might be inclined to advise you that it would be in your interest to cooperate with us now."

Greenway scowled and said coldly, "I would thank you, Chief Inspector, not to presume what advice I might or might not give to my client. Please confine your comments in this interview to relevant matters and facts, not conjecture."

Parker continued, "Well, Jacques?"

"No comment."

"You do not wish to say anything more in your defence?"

"No comment."

"In that case you will remain here, in custody."

"Are you going to charge him, Chief Inspector? And if so, with what?" asked Greenway.

"I will charge him when I am ready to do so, Madam, and you will, of course, be informed of the charges beforehand. This interview is terminated at ten-fourteen a.m."

Twenty-Seven

That evening, Dave Manners put his coat on and joined Pete Lee as they left to go home. "Fancy a pint, Pete?"

"Only if you insist."

"Right, then, you can drive."

They had barely left the car park when Dave's phone rang. "It's the Memsahib. Hello, gorgeous, the boy wonder and I are just on our way. We thought of stopping off for a swift half first, though."

"Well, husband dear, dinner will be ready in about an hour, so don't be late."

"Oh! Steak and kidney pie! Nothing short of a national disaster would make me late for that."

"How do you know it's steak and kidney pie?"

"Because, dearest, I am a detective, didn't I ever tell you that? And besides, you asked me to call into the butchers on my home yesterday and buy some steak and kidney, and I thought that might have been a clue."

"Well, ask the handsome stranger if he would like to share our repast."

He looked at Pete. "Boss lady says to ask Desperate Dan if he would like a portion of cow pie?"

Pete pretended to be horrified. "Oh, please don't make me eat Jean's cooking! Anything but that! I promise to be good, honest!"

"And tell that great lump that I heard that."

"No, no, lovely lady, that wasn't me, that was Sergeant Muffin here practicing his ventriloquist act again."

"I think you had better come straight home, husband dear, before daddy long legs gets into any more trouble."

"Wilco, Honey, we are on our way," then to Peter, "home, James. And you do like to live dangerously, don't you?"

"Well, you know that I am totally fearless when it comes to policing the mean streets of our fair county, but even I am not brave, or foolish, enough to incur the wrath of my favourite pie cook. I will just pull into the forecourt of this convenient garage, which we happen to be approaching, and buy a bunch of flowers."

"And I hope you don't think that a pathetic peace offering like that will ameliorate your troubles with my good lady?"

"Oh no, indeed. That would be a triumph of optimism over experience, but I live in hope! And please don't use those silly long words on me, you know they make my little brain hurt."

They were still giggling like a pair of schoolgirls when Pete pulled onto Dave's drive. As they got out, the door opened to reveal Dave's wife with her hands on her hips and an expression of mock severity on her beautiful face. "Now, look here, boy wonder..." she began.

Pete stooped down and kissed her on the top of her head and thrust the flowers into her hands. "Good evening, lovely lady, you are so kind to invite this humble sleuth to share your dreadful, I mean delightful, cooking. I am indeed a lucky little chap."

"Come on in you great oaf, and don't push your luck."

They hung their coats in the hall and Jean said, "Why don't you go and wash the police station smell off your tiny paws whilst my dear husband tries to remember the combination for his secret cache of beer?"

"You mean the secret cache under the stairs that no one knows about?"

"Let it be our secret, Petey darling."

Both Dave and Peter did full justice to the steak and kidney pie, seconds in the case of Pete, of course, then he said, "Oh, I do hope you are not going to force some of your notorious apple pie on me, Madam?"

"I wouldn't dream of it, Boy Wonder, unless you grovel humbly at my feet."

"Oh, I would, I would, Lovely Lady, it's just that, in my state of health, if I get down on my knees I may never get back up again."

Dave interjected a more serious note, "Pete, what did you think of Chalky's discovery of..."

"Whoa!" said Jean. "Please remember the rules of the house, here. There will be no shop talk here before, during, or after a meal. Dirty jokes if you must, but no shop talk."

Dave and Pete both raised their hands in surrender. "Your wish is our command lovely lady," said Pete.

After a few more bottles had been excavated from Dave's 'secret cache' and more banter, Jean looked at the clock and said, "Boy wonder, there is no way that we law-abiding folk could allow you to drive yourself home tonight, so I suppose we are lumbered with you. You can use our spare room, of course, and, if needs be, I will lend you one of my baby-doll nighties."

"Why, thank you kindly, Ma'am, I would be pleased to accept your gracious offer – of the bed, that is, not your nightie, but only on the condition that you promise not to sneak in in the wee small hours and try to molest me."

***

After a breakfast of toast and Alkaseltzers, they were about to leave the house when Dave's phone rang. It was Parker. "Where are you?"

"Just leaving home, Guv, with my trusty assistant."

"Well, head straight for Kings Dalton. It looks as if Peters has been found. Elder Close is a cul-de-sac off Hawthorne Road. I'll see you at the end of it, number seventeen. Tell Pete to make his way to the station and check on the search reports for Peters' and Jacques' places which, I'm told, will be on my desk."

"OK, Guv, we're on our way." He kissed Jean. "Gotta dash, honey, be good."

"Thanks for the hospitality, little missy, and the awful cordon noire meal, you are a star and I love you to bits," grinned Pete.

"One of these days," said Jean, "someone will take you seriously and then there will be another murder investigation for my poor, overworked husband."

"Poor, overworked husband? Are you admitting to bigamy, madam?" He giggled then gave her a hug, then squeezed himself into the passenger seat of Dave's car and said, "You can drop me at the bus stop if you would be so kind, Sergeant Muffin, Sir."

Twenty-Eight

As he drove into Elder Close, Manners could see Parker's car at the far end, behind a police van and a plain private ambulance. A small, white van had been reversed on to the drive and he assumed, correctly, as it turned out, that it belonged to the tiler who had raised the alarm. Dr. de Vrie's unmistakeable Aston Martin was parked across the end of the close. Jan de Vrie was the police surgeon and pathologist, and Manners was invariably surprised at how he seemed always to be at the scene before anyone else. He tended to refer to him as the 'prescient dutchman' much to the amusement of Jan who hadn't lived in the Netherlands since he was two years old and spoke not a word of Dutch.

Parker met him as he got out of his car and led him round to the back of the building where the scene of crime team were erecting a canvas screen. "Morning, Doc."

"Good morning, gentlemen, we have an interesting one here."

"Yes, indeed," said Parker, "what do you make of it?"

"Well, this young man has a fractured skull with a considerable indentation above, and slightly behind the right ear. For good measure, he has been garrotted with what appears to be a plastic cable tie, but I cannot be sure of that until I can remove it and I cannot do that here. It was pulled very tight, and the flesh has swollen over it, so it will have to wait until I can get him on the table."

"His posture looks strange, don't you think?" asked Parker. "With his head turned in against the wheel like that? Could that be where the fracture came from?"

"Oh, no, definitely not, but I agree it *is* strange. If he had received a blow like that whilst he was sitting or standing astride the bike, he couldn't have fallen with his head so close to the wheel, and whoever struck him would have been standing on the other side of the bike."

"Yet he hadn't dismounted because his right leg is still draped over the saddle," observed Manners.

"Quite so," agreed de Vrie. "As far as I can see, the angle of the blow would suggest that it was administered when he was stooped down, almost against the side of the bike, but his head must have been turned in towards it."

"Now what could have caused him to be in a position like that do you suppose?" mused Parker.

"I have no idea, you are the detectives, or so I'm told."

Parker grinned. "Any idea what might have caused the blow then?"

"It's difficult to say, not your usual 'blunt instrument' for sure, but something quite large and round. Again, I will have a better idea after the P.M."

"And his ponytail has been caught in the front wheel. That couldn't have been accidental when he fell, surely?"

"Highly unlikely in my view, and most certainly the garrotting wasn't accidental."

"How long has he been dead, would you say Doc?" asked Manners.

"I'll tell you that when I've completed the P.M., but if you want a rough figure, and I'm sure you do, then I would say at least forty-eight hours and probably a bit more."

"Thank you."

"Well, I think I have accomplished all that I can here. If you would arrange for him to be brought in for me when you have finished, I'll try to arrange the P.M. for this afternoon. Will you or young David here wish to be present?"

"Not if I can possibly avoid it," grinned Dave, "but we'll let you know."

As Dr. Vrie left, Parker turned to the constable who had been the first on the scene in response to the 999 call. "Who found the body, constable?"

"A Mr, Phelps, Sir. He is waiting just inside this back door here. He is a tiler and arrived just after seven-thirty this morning to work in the kitchen. He is a 'trying-to-give-up-smoker' and came out the back door to have a quick drag before starting work and saw this lot. As soon as he had finished vomiting, he called 999 at," he checked his notebook, "seven-thirty-eight. I was the nearest patrol and arrived on the scene at seven-fifty-two."

"Thank you. Go and get a statement from him Dave while I check with the photographer to make sure he has all the shots we want, then I'll come and join you. Meanwhile, constable, you stay here and guard the scene. I will be here also until the body is removed, then the SOCO will give you any further instructions."

"Very good, Sir."

***

Manners let himself in through the back door to see the tiler, as white as a sheet, sitting on a pile of boxes of wall tiles. He had a thermos flask cup in his hand and was smoking feverishly. "I shall probably get the boot for smoking in here, but Christ, that was awful."

"Hello. I'm Detective Sergeant Manners and you are Mr. Phelps?"

"Yeah, Sean Phelps."

"And you found the body and called 999, is that right?"

Phelps nodded and took another drag on his cigarette.

"Would you tell me exactly what happened please?"

"I already told your mate out there."

"Yes, but I'd like you to go over it again with me. Then I can take your statement and leave you in peace, although you will have to leave here as it will be classed as a 'scene of crime'. Of course, we could do this at the station if you would prefer?"

"No, no, I just want to get away from here and sod the tiling. I don't think I could work here now anyway."

"Very understandable, Sir. Now can you just confirm your name and address for me?"

"Sean Phelps." He gave an address in Elmington.

"And are you employed by the developers here as a tiler?"

"Oh no. I'm self-employed. I run my own business and employ two other tilers and a young lad who is learning the trade. I have a contract for a third of the premises on this development, but that includes all the bungalows in Elder Close and most of the finished houses in Hawthorne Road. This one though, I think, will have to be done by Eric, or Fred. I don't think I could stomach it anymore."

"What time did you arrive on site here this morning, Sean? Is it OK if I call you Sean?"

"Sure. Just about half seven I would guess; it was just getting light. I unloaded the van, brought all the boxes in and all the gear. I started to mark up the wall over the sink then thought I would have a quick smoke before I got my hands all mucky. The developers are absolutely nuts about not smoking in any of the building once the walls have gone up, so I went out the back door here, and at first I just saw the bike. I thought it was a bit odd for a bike to be parked round the back, especially as none of the props at this end are occupied. Anyway, I got a little closer to it and saw the bloke there. I went to see if he was alright, or perhaps fallen off or something, but his face was all blue and his eyes were staring. Christ, mate, I nearly messed meself, I can tell you. Well, I was as sick as a dog, but I turned away a bit first. Then I rang 999 on my mobile and they told me to stay here until the Police arrived. And I can tell you they were here a damn sight quicker than they were when I reported that my shed had been broken into and two hundred-and-fifty quid's worth of tiles nicked!"

"How did you let yourself in here?"

"I collected the front door key from the Estate Office; normal practice, we have to sign for it then keep it until we have finished the job. The keys to the back door and utility boxes etc are left in the kitchen, and always in the drawer furthest from the door. Regular routine for any of the workers whether they are employees or sub-contractors."

"Did you see any other vehicles along this end of the Close? Or anyone walking around?"

"No, the place was deserted. Even the ones that are occupied at the other end showed no sign of getting about."

"Thank you, Sean, you have been most helpful. Now, if I just write up what you have told me, I'll get you to sign it and you can be off. It is possible that we might need to talk to you again, but I think not very likely – you have been very clear."

***

Manners came out of the back door and stood looking at the bike and body for a few minutes. He walked slowly round the bike, then pulled on a pair of plastic gloves and carefully lifted the crash helmet from where it hung on the handlebars. It was old and well-worn with plenty of scratches across the top. He turned it over in his hands, but the inside was greasy and the lining ragged. Looking at the outside again something caught his eye; he pulled a small, folding magnifier from his pocket and saw what appeared to be a small cluster of hairs stuck to the surface. He called to Parker, "Guv, I think we may have found the source of that dent in his head. There are a few hairs stuck to the top of this helmet and by the look of them they could well belong to this chap." He called one of the SOCO team over and asked him to bag the helmet for forensic examination.

Parker frowned. "But how could his assailant have got hold of his helmet, made him stoop down, as de Vrie suggests, and be in a position to belt him without arousing his suspicion? Peters must have given him the helmet and bent down to look at something in all innocence. Curiouser and curiouser!"

"If it's all right with you, Guv, I'd like to get back and see what Lee has found in those search reports."

"Good idea, Dave, I will finish off here, then come and join you. Gather as many of the crew as you can together in the incident room, I want a briefing and a brain-storming session as soon as I get there. And see if you can get Carter and Walters to join us; their boss is Inspector Forbes of the uniformed mob, his phone number is in the book on my desk; he's normally pretty reasonable but if you have a problem ring me."

"OK, Guv, but you'd better move your car a bit to let our tiler get off the drive, I think he's rather keen to get away from here."

Twenty-Nine

The incident room was becoming more crowded each time a briefing was called. Manners had arranged for George Carter to attend but Tony Walters was giving evidence in Court on an unrelated case, so could not be present. He had collected the Search Reports from Lee and they were discussing them prior to the arrival of DCI Parker. "Yes, indeed, Pete, these certainly are interesting, I'd like to share these with 'Nosey' before he starts now. And I think the brain-storming session might prove to be lively."

He caught Parker's attention as he came in and went into his office where he showed him the search reports. "No surprises as far as the drugs are concerned, Dave, but these other bits put brother Jacques in a different light, don't they?"

They both returned to the incident room where Parker called for attention. "Before we start, I'd like to welcome P.C. George Carter to our happy throng. He and Tony Walters shared guard duty on Denton's door in the Hospital and he may well have more information for us. His boss is Inspector Forbes, and he has kindly agreed that George can stay seconded to us for as long as this takes. So please make him welcome and I don't want to hear any juvenile crap about 'wooden tops', got it?"

There was general mutterings and nods of acknowledgement to George, then Parker continued, "Sergeant Manners and I will bring you up to date on the latest events and the search reports, then I want a brain-storming session. If you have anything to say, that will be the time. Any ideas, doubts or suggestions, don't hold back. I want to hear them all. Firstly, though, I have to tell you that the body of 'Zack' Peters was found this morning, together with his motor bike in a cul-de-sac in the Adlands farm development in Kings Dalton. Dave?"

Manners gave a detailed account of the finding of Peters and of what evidence there was.

"So, now," said Parker, "we have two murders; Denton and Peters. We are almost certain that Denton was one of the three that attacked the Flemings, and from the description given by Mr. Fleming and Mr. Mason, the cyclist who came to their aid, there is a high probability that Peters was one of the others with Denton at that time. That raises some interesting points regarding Colin Jacques. But before we get to that, I would like you to hear the results of the searches carried out on the properties of Messrs Peters and Jacques."

**

He nodded at Phil Pearson. "Phil, I believe you oversaw the search at Hadley Court Road?"

"Yes, Guv. As we suspected there was quite a stash of drugs, with much already cut and put into foil screws – forty-eight of them actually, and they appeared to be identical to the screw that was found on Denton when he was admitted to Elmington General. There was a supermarket zip-lock freezer bag hidden under a chest of drawers in the bedroom which contained three thousand eight hundred and forty pounds, all in used notes and all pretty grubby. There was something about the motor bike, though, that worried me. Did he have the V5 with him when you found him, Guv?"

"V5? You mean the vehicle registration certificate? No, he didn't."

"Well, that is strange. It might have meant that he didn't actually own the bike, but there were tax, MOT and insurance documents in his name, albeit they were about eighteen months out of date, but he couldn't have taxed it without a V5 and it's not the sort of thing that you would carry around with you – unless..."

"Unless?" said Parker.

"A thought that just occurred to me," said Pearson, "unless he was taking it somewhere to sell it."

"Now, that is a good point," said Manners. "If he thought that his assailant was a prospective buyer, he might well have stooped to look at an apparent problem on the engine, say, which would cause his head to be where Doc de Vrie thought it could be when he was clobbered."

"Yes, but we are making a lot of assumptions here. Let's leave that for a moment. Was there anything else, Phil?"

"Yes, we didn't find a passport, either. I was about to check with the passport office at Newport to see if he had ever been issued with one."

"Good thinking, Phil, and thank you. Sunni?"

***

Sunni Patel had led the search team at Jacques' house and now had a grin on his face. "Yes, Guv, and there seems to be more to our Colin Jacques than might at first be apparent. There was a lot of drugs; what looked like fairly high-grade heroin, total weight seven and a half kilograms, so somewhat more than he could claim for personal use. There was also all the associated paraphernalia we would expect of a dealer. We found a box under the bath with thirty-four thousand, two hundred pounds in cash. There was a small notebook in the bag as well and that had lots of entries that looked very much like his drug dealing records. Just initials, dates and amounts. 'ZP', or sometimes just 'Z' appears fairly often, and I assume that is Peters. The amount against his name is invariable about two hundred pounds whereas the others are usually in the high hundreds or a thousand at a time. It is also with forensics at the moment, but as soon as we get it back, I would like to try and trace some of those initials."

"Yes, you do that, please," said Parker, "and?"

"There were other items in his bedroom which I will come to in a moment, but first, I managed to draw the short straw and got the job of searching his rubbish bins. He didn't have one for the garden waste, just the recycling one for papers, glass and tins, etc. and one for general rubbish. And it was this latter that produced the jackpot. I found a half empty plastic bottle of hair colouring mousse, darkish brown, called 'chilli chocolate' of all things! It is the temporary sort that can be washed out easily. I then spotted a small plastic case which I recognised instantly because my wife has one just the same. It was a case for contact lenses. But this one didn't contain your normal prescription contact lenses, oh no Sir. This one contained *tinted* lenses – bright blue tinted lenses." He paused for effect. "Then Sunni continues with even more of his renowned enthusiasm and I found some small pieces of coloured card which had been cut up but, when pieced together, form an almost complete identity badge with the NHS logo in the top left corner and the name Sinclair, not quite complete, across the centre. It looked like it had been made of photo paper and stuck onto cardboard, but our forensic boys have it and the lenses, of course, for finger printing, etc.

"But there is one thing Guv that isn't on my report and that is because it didn't mean anything to me at the time, but now that Sergeant Manners has given us the details of Peters' demise, well, I searched his van of course, the back doors and the passenger door were all locked, but the driver's door wasn't. The back contained some bags of cement and plaster, a couple of step stools and a power 'paddle mixer', all as we might expect of a plasterer. *But...*" again the pause for effect, "under the front seat was a newish packet of large plastic cable ties! Not usually associated with the gentle art of plastering, I think."

Parker looked up. "Cable ties? Where are they, then?"

"Still in the van, Sir, of course. I had no reason to think they could be of interest. I did, naturally, lock the van and I believe that it was brought into our garage for close examination by the forensic team. It strikes me now, though, that the bag of ties was about the only thing in the van that wasn't covered with cement dust and plaster."

"Well done, Sunni, now get hold of that pack of ties and see if you can identify where they came from."

"Oh, that's easy, Guv, it's Screwbase. Their name is on almost everything they sell. For the benefit of the non-DIYers amongst us, Screwbase is a sort of tool supermarket with hundreds of branches all over the country and interestingly enough, when you buy something from them, even if it's only a box of screws or a paint brush, they ask you for your name and address, and email, if you have one, so that they can plague you with advertising junk forevermore. So, the chances are good that they will have a record of the buyer – can't have sold too many packets of large cable ties in the last month, I would have thought."

"Good thinking, Sunni, get the bag to forensics and check out Screwbase, and with some priority, right?"

"Right, Guv."

"Now the other 'items of interest' that were found in his bedroom? What of them? I have feeling that this is where your stupid grin fits in, perhaps?"

"Ah, yes, Guv. In various drawers in Mr. Jacques' bedroom, at least I assume it was his bedroom as it was the only one of the two rooms described as bedrooms that had a bed in it."

"Oh, for heaven's sake, cut the crap and get on with it."

"Yes, Guv, of course." He grinned. "Well, as I say, in various drawers in said bedroom there was an assortment of sex toys. Now, I am, I assure you, no expert on these things, so I had to resort to friend Google to identify them for me. They comprised," he made much of consulting his notes, "two vibrating dildos, two rattan canes, three assorted spanking paddles and several containers of, er, 'Love Lubricant'. The fact that there were two of most of these, er, things would suggest that they were possibly not for his singular amusement but, well, 'two's company' they say, although Jacques is the sole owner, and apparent occupier, of those premises. And that, I think, Sir, completes my search report!"

"Thank you, Sunni, and for Crissakes stop looking so damned smug!"

Sunni sat down amid a burst of applause and a few rude innuendos from his colleagues, which he acknowledged with a slight bow and an even sillier grin.

Thirty

"Right," said Parker, "let us now consider the implications of these latest events, and I want some thoughts from you lot. The discovery of Peters, for a start. Bearing in mind that we think – no proof, of course – that he was one of Denton's accomplices in the attack on the Flemings, that suggests that Jacques could himself be at risk *if* he was the third member of the group *and* these were revenge killings. That is a thought that I will certainly put to Jacques when we next interview him. Yes, Pete, you want to chip in?"

"I do, Guv, it also suggests the possibility that, if revenge is not the motive, Brother Jacques could have knocked off Denton *and* Peters."

"Why would he want to do that? They were his mates, if not his actual accomplices," said Corbett.

"Because," said Lee, "there was a risk that they would have named him as a participant in what has turned out to be a manslaughter case, and he had a lot to lose. With his record he would almost certainly go down for a long time if convicted, and he wouldn't want to chance that. And consider this: he is about the right build as our Sinclair imposter and coloured hair mousse and contact lenses were found in his rubbish bin, together with bits of what could prove to be a false identity tab matching that which George saw on Sinclair."

"Yes," said Sunni, "*if* forensics find his DNA or fingerprints on any of them, otherwise they are circumstantial at best."

Lee continued, "I accept that Sunni certainly, but even if there were no fingerprints, those items would need some explaining away. Also, he would have known that Denton was in hospital, and it would not have taken too much to find which one and which ward, would it?"

"A good hypothesis, Pete," said Parker, "but when Dave and I interviewed him, he didn't strike me as being very intelligent. I wonder if he would have the ability to impersonate a surgeon with enough conviction to convince both George, who I think is not an easy man to fool, and the nurse on the ward. And could he have known how to inject air into Denton's vein and, indeed, the implications of doing that?"

"Well, Guv," interrupted Watson, "considering his involvement in the drug scene, I would have thought that injections of any sort would be second nature to him. And, if it was him, Denton would have been likely to let him fiddle with his cannula if he thought that his mate was going to give him some of the drugs that he was beginning to crave for."

"Good point, Beryl, but would Denton have recognised him as his mate? After all, whoever it was had gone to some considerable lengths *not* to look like himself."

"And," said Corbett, "your opinion of his intellect would account for him being stupid enough to leave a lot of evidence in his rubbish bin when it was pretty obvious that we would search it."

"If it was him who put it in the bin," said Parker.

"OK, then," said Manners, "if it wasn't Jacques, who are the alternatives? As I see it there are four choices: one, Richard Fleming, who, if these *were* revenge killings, has the strongest possible motive, but in my opinion, lacks the necessary physical ability. He is, as I've already pointed out, seventy-eight years of age, is fairly frail and walks only with the aid of a stick. Two, Richard's son, Tony. His motive for revenge would probably be almost as strong as his dad's, but he lives at least an hour's drive away, although he could well have done the Sinclair charade, if he fits physically and we haven't seen him so can't confirm that. Three, Arthur Mason, a very long shot, though. He is the cyclist who intervened in the assault on the Flemings and saved them a lot of grief. I mention him only because he was involved in the incident, but I can't see any possible motive for him to get involved to this extent. He was no more than a passing Samaritan. And four of course would be someone else. Person or persons unknown, as they say."

"There is a point here, Guv," said Pete. "It's just a thought, but when Dave and I called on Arthur Mason we asked if his wife was there, and he said that he had lost her. I noticed a framed poster on his wall for the Elmington Players production of the Pirates of Penzance. I noticed it because I'm rather keen on a spot of Gilbert and Sullivan and the Pirates is one of my favourites. The production though was about a couple of years ago and I wondered if perhaps he trod the boards as they say and might have been in it. But being it was framed and in a fairly prominent position in the house I thought it might have been his wife that was in it. There was a framed photograph of his wife on his mantleshelf, and she looked a very attractive lady. I didn't like to ask too much as it didn't seem relevant, but if he is a thespian and if we are looking for an impostor who acted the part of a visiting surgeon?"

"Thanks, Pete," said Parker, "that may well be worth following up. So where does that leave us? Richard, and indeed Tony Fleming, would have known that Denton had been admitted to a hospital, but not which one. The Sinclair imposter *knew* which hospital, *and* which ward he was in, so how did he know that?

"George, was there anyone in the ward, however earlier, who could have been sussing out the place? Or was there any activity which, with hindsight, might have been unusual or odd in any way?"

George Carter frowned and started thumbing through his notebook. "Nothing springs to mind, Sir, I was very aware of the need to identify any unusual or suspicious activity or interest in the ward, but everyone who was in, or went in, seemed to have a good reason. And if anyone had gone in who wasn't expected or recognised, they would have been challenged by the sister or nurses straight away. Obviously, I didn't record all the nurses, etc. individually, but I did record those others but, as I've said, there was no one that seemed not to have a valid reason for being there or for doing what they did. Let me just re-cap, if I may?"

"Please do."

Carter read from his notebook. "On the day of Denton's death, then, apart from nurses and doctors there were two physiotherapists, the cleaner, the tea wallah, the water girl and the meal server, sometimes the meals would be delivered by a nurse, sometimes an auxiliary and all these were daily and fairly regular as regards times. In addition, on that day there was a phlebotomist. On my first day there was, additionally, a visit from a pharmacist."

"A pharmacist? You didn't mention a pharmacist."

"Well, he wasn't there on the day in question, he only called the once. It is normal procedure for the hospital pharmacy to send one of their staff round the wards to check on new admissions to make sure that they have an adequate stock of any medication that has been prescribed."

"And?"

"There were only two admissions on that occasion, apart from Denton, there was a builder who had apparently fallen off a building and broken his shoulder. The pharmacist went into Denton's room but didn't close the door, so I watched what he did. He just introduced himself to Denton who, incidentally, ignored him as he did most people, then he read Denton's notes and made a record of them on his phone or whatever it was he had, then did the same for the builder and left."

"Did you check on him?"

"No, Sir, I saw no need to, the nurses all gave the impression that it was a regular and normal procedure."

"Anyone else?"

"Not on my shifts, Sir, no."

"Did you record his name, by any chance?"

"Of course, I did." He glanced at his note book. "He was Roger Newman, BPharm Pharmacist from the hospital pharmacy. Nothing untoward about that or about him as far as I could see."

"OK, George, but if someone had to find out if a damaged leg case had been admitted, and where, and who he was, that might have been a way."

"What? By impersonating a pharmacist, you mean?"

"Not very likely, I agree, but possible. Check him out, would you?"

"Will do, Sir."

"And don't keep calling me Sir. Now that you're on the team, 'Guv' will do."

"OK, Guv, and thanks."

"Right, then, any other thoughts, people? No? OK. To recap. Sunni, you'll check on Screwbase about the cable ties, and that notebook as soon as we get it back, Phil, you will check the passport office to see if there was ever one issued for Peters, and George, you'll check on Newman. And I want answers on those three at tomorrow's briefing. Dave, you and I will have another chat with friend Jacques and Pete, would you check on Richard Fleming again, and make sure that he really is reliant on that stick for his mobility, and find out what you can about his son. Ronnie, check on Arthur Mason, look into his background etc and look into his connections with the Elmington Players. Beryl, I want you to check into Jacques' background a bit more, especially his finances etc. Next briefing, same time tomorrow. OK, then, let's get on with it."

Thirty-One

Helen Greenway had been advised by Manners that they intended to interview Jacques again, and she called into DCI Parker's office for a briefing. She made copious notes of the evidence that had been accrued by the search teams and was also brought up to date regarding Peters and the subsequent murder enquiry. She asked to see Jacques alone before he was formally interviewed and was accompanied to his cell. "Please call me when you are ready to leave," said the uniformed PC as he closed the cell door but stayed in sight, if not in hearing of them. After some fifteen minutes she indicated that she was ready to leave. The PC radioed to DCI Parker then led Jacques up to the interview room where he remained until Parker and Manners arrived and told him to wait outside.

Once seated, Manners switched on the recorder and ran through the introductory preliminaries again. Parker opened a folder on the table and said, "Mr. Jacques, I would remind you that you are still under caution, do you understand that?"

"Yeah."

"Right, where were you on the evening of the twenty-second between eight p.m. and ten?"

Jacques frowned. "Why?"

"Just answer the question."

"No comment."

"Where were you on the twenty-fifth between the hours of four p.m. and seven p.m.?"

"No comment."

"Then let me tell you where I think you were. On the twenty-second at about nine p.m., I think you entered Bolton Ward in Elmington General Hospital whilst impersonating a doctor, and there you entered a private room where your friend and accomplice Harry Denton was. And there, Mr. Jacques, I think you unlawfully killed said Mr. Denton."

"What? What are you on about? Are you saying that Harry is dead?"

"I am indeed, and I am also saying that I think you killed him."

Jacques looked at his solicitor. "What's he saying? I ain't killed no-one. Is Harry really dead? What's he trying to pull here?"

Greenway raised her hand to quieten him, then looked at DCI Parker. "Chief Inspector?"

"Somebody, about your build, had dyed his hair brown, wore coloured contact lenses and had a fake ID card pinned to his white coat and, in an attempt to impersonate a doctor, entered Mr. Denton's room in Bolton Ward and killed him, Mr. Jacques. And, during a search of your premises, various items of interest were found in your rubbish bin. These included a partially-used bottle of brown hair colouring, some tinted contact lenses and some remnants of an obviously false ID card purporting to belong to a hospital doctor. So, you can understand why I think that might be you, Mr. Jacques?"

"You bastard! You planted that stuff! I've never had any hair dye, nor any of that other stuff." He turned to Greenway. "You can't let them do this, they're trying to fit me up for murder for Crissakes. You've got to do something."

There was a knock on the door, and it opened a crack. "Sir?"

"What is it?"

"D.C. Patel wishes to speak to DCI Parker, Sir."

"Is it important?"

"D.C. Patel says that it is, yes, Sir."

"Well, it had better be." He nodded to Manners who spoke into the recorder. "DCI Parker is leaving the room temporarily."

***

When the door closed behind Parker, he leaned forward and said, "Well, there is something else you might like to consider – we are pretty sure that Harry Denton was involved in a mugging that took place in Harpers Lane, Kings Dalton, on Tuesday the fifteenth of this month. And from the descriptions we have from some witnesses, we believe your friend 'Zack' Peters was an accomplice in that attack and so, Mr. Jacques, were you."

"That's balls, I've told you I weren't there, and..."

"Hear me out please," continued Manners. "Now, both Denton and Peters are dead. And it occurs to us that if you didn't kill Denton then possibly, just possibly, someone, perhaps with revenge on their mind, has killed two of the three participants in that attack and that, Mr. Jacques, could leave you in a very vulnerable position. You could be number three on this persons list, don't you see?"

The blood drained from Jacques' face and beads of sweat formed on his forehead. "Jesus! But I told you I wasn't there."

"Oh yes, you told *us*, but then it's not *us* that might be killing off the three muggers, is it?"

Jacques licked his lips and turned to Helen Greenway for inspiration. She remained impassive.

"Of course," continued Manners, "if you were there and we

thought that you were at risk we might be able to offer you Police protection, but naturally there would be no point in us doing that if you weren't there."

Jacques was shaking and his right knee was bouncing up and down. "But *if*, and I do mean *if*, I said that I was there, but didn't take any part in the mugging, you would still charge me, right?"

"We most certainly would, yes."

"And what would the charge be?"

"That would be up to DCI Parker, but I think at least it would be aggravated robbery, and the Court would decide if it was cat one, that of course is where serious harm is caused to the victim, or it could be manslaughter, because, as I'm sure your solicitor has told you, Mrs. Mary Fleming, one of the victims has subsequently died as a direct result of the attack. So, I won't lie to you, Mr. Jacques, you will be facing serious charges. You may consider, though, that that could be a preferable alternative to looking over your shoulder in fear for the rest of your life."

Helen Greenway interrupted. "That is enough of that, Sergeant, that is coercion, and I will not permit it."

"Not at all, madam, I am merely trying to let your client know the situation as I see it, so that he can make an informed decision regarding his course of action. With the aid of your advice, of course."

***

As DCI Parker left the interview room, he was confronted by Sunni Patel who had a sheet of paper in his hand and was shifting his weight from one foot to the other in a rare display of impatience. "Sorry to interrupt, Guv, but I thought I should bring this to your attention sooner rather than later."

"What is it, Sunni?"

"It's the cable ties, Sir. Screwbase have come up trumps on this for me. As I said in the briefing, they record the names and addresses of all their customers whenever they can, and..."

"Yes, yes, I know. Just get on with it."

"Guv. Well, in the last month they sold only four packs of large cable ties from their Elmington store, two of them were to large Electrical Contractors and one to a small one-man electrician, all three of whom have accounts with them. But the other sale was to a Mr. Colin Jacques of thirty-four Preston Way, Kings Dalton, for cash on the twenty-fifth of this month at ten-thirty-seven a.m."

Parker clapped him on the shoulder. "Well done, Sunni. I assume that Screwbase could provide the evidence for that?"

"Indeed, yes, at the moment I have only word of mouth from one of their customer service chaps at their head office, but I have his name and he has promised to send me a hard copy of the receipt within the hour, and they would be prepared to give evidence in court if that should be necessary."

"Thank you, Sunni, you have done well, so I will excuse your revoltingly smug look this time. But only for this time, you understand."

"Thank you, Guv. You have just made Sunni Patel one very happy DC person."

Parker took the paper from him and re-entered the interview room. As he took his seat, Manners announced his return for the benefit of the tape then said, "Mr. Jacques is just considering, Sir, whether to admit that he took part in the mugging in Harpers Lane."

"Thank you, Sergeant, but first, Mr. Jacques I would like you to think back to my original question; where were you on the evening of Tuesday the twenty-second and the afternoon of Friday the twenty-fifth of this month? And please think very carefully before you answer."

Jacques was now shaking uncontrollably as he turned to Greenway. "These bastards are trying to fit me up for murder, you can see that. Can't you stop them for Crissakes?"

"I'm afraid that we have to listen to what they have to say," she replied, "but they will be aware that they have very few minutes left of their twenty-four hours before they need either to charge or release you. But I really think that you should tell them where you were on that Tuesday evening."

"Do I have to?"

"They are likely to charge you with murder, for heaven's sake, and you have a positive and verifiable alibi – of course you should tell them!"

Parker ignored her and said to Jacques, "I have told you what I think you were doing on the evening of the twenty-second but, what were you doing on the afternoon or early evening of the twenty-fifth? As you won't tell us I will tell you. We have evidence that you unlawfully killed Cecil John Peters, A.K.A. Zack, by garrotting him with a plastic cable tie, or rather with three ties to be exact, and that a packet of ties, which I am sure forensics will be able to confirm, contained the ties that were found around the neck of Peters, was found under the passenger seat of your van, and we have evidence that you purchased them from the Elmington branch of Screwbase at ten-thirty-seven on the twenty-fifth of this month, the day before the said Cecil John Peters was garrotted to death. Now what do you say, Mr. Jacques?"

"This is bloody ridiculous, you planted that. I've not been in Screwbase for yonks." He looked down in dismay at the wet stain appearing on the front of his trousers and squirmed. Helen Greenway said, "Will you tell them or do I have to?"

He stared at the tabletop and said, in a shaky voice, "I was at the New Moon Club from about eight until nearly half past ten."

"The New Moon?" said Manners. "The gay night club?"

"Yeah."

"And is there anyone who can vouch for you there?"

He looked pleadingly at Greenway. "Go on tell them."

"The barman of course, but I was there with Tim all evening. He was there first, though."

"Tim? And does Tim have a surname?

"I suppose."

"You suppose? You don't know? So, was this Tim just a one-night stand then?"

"Sergeant! I object most strongly to your homophobic attitude. I would be obliged if you would just let my client tell you what he needs to in his own way. This is difficult enough for him without your snide implications."

"Right, so let me put it another way, was Tim just a casual acquaintance or had you met him before?"

"Of course, I had, we were friends."

"But you don't know his name, other than Tim?"

"That's all I ever called him. No one ever uses surnames much in the Moon."

"OK, so you left there at about ten-thirty?"

"Yeah. I said."

"Alone?"

He glanced at Greenway again who nodded. "No, Tim came home with me, for a coffee and nightcap, like."

"And what time did Tim leave?"

Another glance at Greenway, another rather impatient nod.

"About seven the next morning."

"Oh, I see," said Manners, "and where could we find Tim? You know his address, I presume?"

"No. We only ever meet at the New Moon, Tuesdays and Fridays."

"They are the only nights that Tim is there?"

"No, it's the only nights that I go."

"So, describe him for me."

He gave a detailed description which Manners thought would be good enough to enable him to be recognised, and on a nod from Parker, agreed to visit the New Moon to try and locate him.

"So, what about Friday the twenty-fifth?" asked Parker. "Were you at the New Moon then as well?"

"Yeah, but not until about eight o'clock."

"Then where were you from, say, four until then?"

"I was working until six on the new estate at Palmington and that's about half an hour's drive to get home, then I had a shower and a bite to eat and got ready to go to the Moon."

"And what work was that, exactly?"

"I'm a Plasterer, self-employed, but I am contracted to Ball and Co. who are the main constructors at the Palmington development."

"Anyone vouch for you there?"

"No, I was on my own. I've got a lad who usually helps but he tested positive for COVID, so he had to isolate."

"Are you satisfied now, Chief Inspector?" asked Greenway.

"If we can find this Tim person, and if he confirms your client's story, then possibly. But as I am aware of the time, Mr. Jacques, you may go for the time being, but please do not try to leave the country."

Manners announced the closing routine to the tape, then switched off the recorder, removed the tapes and signed them. He put his hand on Jacques' shoulder and said, "Allow me to accompany you to the Custody Sergeant, Mr. Jacques, where you can sign for your belongings and bid your farewell. Meanwhile, I believe that Chief Inspector Parker would like a word with your legal adviser here."

Thirty-Two

Jacques checked the contents of the envelope containing his possessions; keys, mobile phone, a roll of bank notes held by an elastic band and some small change, all of which he made an elaborate show of counting, before signing the receipt form offered by the Custody Sergeant. He put his possessions in his pocket and turned to leave. He had gone no more than three paces when a figure blocked his path. He looked up to see a smiling Asian man in a plaid jumper holding up a Warrant Card. "Colin Frederick Jacques, I am Detective Constable Patel, and I am arresting you for possession of a quantity of a class-A drugs with intent to supply. You do not have to say anything, but it may harm your defence if you do not mention when questioned something which you later rely on in court. Anything you do say may be given in evidence. Do you understand?"

Jacques' jaw dropped and he tried to take a step backwards only to bump into something that felt like a brick wall, then two huge hands clamped around his elbows and a large shaven head appeared over his shoulder. "Just not your day, is it, Colin old son?" said Peter Lee without a trace of a smile.

"If you would just turn around, we can go back to the desk where that nice Custody Sergeant has something to say to you," said Sunni as Lee turned him and pushed him towards the desk. "This is Colin Frederick Jacques, Sergeant. He is to be charged with possession of a quantity of class-A drugs with intent to supply, if you would be so kind. I have already cautioned him."

The Custody Sergeant looked at him impassively. "Empty your pockets, please." Then, as Jacques tried to get his hands in his pockets with Lee's hands still clamped round his elbows, said, "Who is the arresting officer?"

"That would be me, Sarge, D.C. Sunni Patel."

Thirty-Three

Manners parked his car about a hundred yards from the entrance to the New Moon Club and walked towards the steps leading up to the door, which opened as he approached to reveal a large doorman in a tight-fitting jacket over a black turtle-neck T-shirt.
"Card?"
"What card?"
"Membership card. This is a members' only club."
Manners held up his warrant card. "This is the only card I need, now open the door, please."
The doorman looked closely at it then stepped back to allow Manners into the small entrance hall. He closed the door then pressed a switch on the wall. Immediately the large, padded door behind Manners opened and a blast of music hit him like a physical blow.
"Who's the Landlord?"
"Jonny. You'll find him behind the bar by the gin rack."
The room in which he found himself was about thirty feet wide and at least twice that long. An elaborate bar ran almost the entire length of the wall opposite the door. The wall behind it was covered with illuminated mirrors and glass shelves supporting a variety of bottles. In the centre was a long row of optics at least fourteen of which held varieties of gin; the gin rack, Manners assumed. Against the wall opposite the bar were little alcoves each containing a small table and two chairs, and yet more wall mirrors. The divisions between the alcoves were of polished

wood and etched glass, each about five feet high. Privacy, of a sort, he supposed. At the far end of the room was a small dance floor facing a stage on which a DJ was gibbering unintelligibly into a microphone.

The lights in the room were gradually cycling between pink and purple and a small glitter ball over the dance area was scattering multi-coloured spots of light around the entire room which were flickering in time with the beat of the music. There was a dozen or more men leaning on the bar and about half of the tables were occupied. Five or six couples were on the dance floor, most slowly moving together and holding each other in various forms of embrace.

Manners made his way over to the bar where a young man with a purple Mohican hair cut was polishing glasses.

"Jonny?"

"Who wants him?"

Manners held up his Warrant Card. "I do."

The lad nodded towards a tall man in a white T-shirt, with the logo of the New Moon printed on the front, further along the bar. "That's 'im."

The Landlord looked up as Manners approached him. "What can I do for you, Inspector?"

"Inspector? What makes you think I'm a policeman?"

"I clocked you as soon as you came through the door, and I can spot the long arm of the law at fifty paces. Part of my job, mate."

"OK, but I'm a Sergeant, not an Inspector."

"All the same to me."

"Are you Jonny?"

"I am."

"And you are in charge of this, er, establishment?"

"I am."

"Can we go somewhere a little quieter where we can talk? I can't hear myself think here."

"That would depend on what you want to talk about."

"Well, the renewal of your trading and alcohol licences for a start, and possibly a forensic audit of your books, and perhaps to arrange a suitable time for a drug squad raid on these premises. Would that do for starters?"

"All right, no need for all that."

"Then stop acting the smart arse and let's go and talk sensibly somewhere."

"Just a moment, then." He put his hand to his right ear, in which was a fitting that could have been a hearing aid but probably wasn't. "Estelle, can you come out here and take over for a moment?"

A door in the back wall between the rows of optics opened and Estelle appeared. She, or more likely he, thought Manners, wore fishnet tights, a short, flared skirt, a leather bodice and shoulder-length hair dyed green and orange; fake eye lashes heavy with mascara and over-applied rouge with a garish red lipstick all conspired to make a caricature of the face.

"Keep an eye on this end of the bar for a while, dear," said Jonny, then led Manners through the door behind the bar and into a small, but elegantly furnished, office. The sound of the music stopped immediately, leaving Manners impressed at the efficiency of the sound proofing.

Jonny sat in a high backed, leather swivel chair behind the desk and waved Manners to one of the small, upholstered chairs in front of it. "Take a seat, Sergeant, I'm sorry about the charade out there, but it wouldn't do for my customers to get the impression that the police were too welcome here, hmm?"

Manners passed across a photograph of Jacques. "Do you recognise this man?"

"Of course, that's Colin. A regular on Tuesdays and Fridays if memory serves."

"Has he been a member long?"

"Many years. I couldn't say just how many off-hand, but I could look it up if you wish."

"That might not be necessary for the moment. Do you have a member called Tim-something?"

"Yes, indeed. Colin is one of Tim's friends."

"One of his friends? Does Tim have many 'friends' then?"

Jonny grinned. "Not an enemy in the world, Sergeant."

"So can you tell me if Colin and Tim were both here on the evening of the twenty-second?"

"Oh yes, for sure. Of course, I can't say for certain what time they arrived or left, but they would have been here. Their's is a pretty constant routine, and usually Colin arrives about eight and they leave together just after ten."

"Ever any trouble with them?"

"Not after a slight misunderstanding shortly after he became a member."

"And what was that about?"

"They were both sitting in one of the alcoves opposite the bar when they started fumbling with each other. I was over there in about three seconds flat and politely explained that that sort of behaviour is totally unacceptable in here."

"Fumbling? Unacceptable? In here?"

"I take exception to that homophobic attitude, Sergeant."

"I am not homophobic, I am merely trying to get the facts and form an opinion of two of your customers. So, there is no need for you to get so defensive."

"All right, then, but yes, that sort of behaviour is strictly out of order in this club. If that were allowed to continue, than one thing leads to another, and I have no intention of being accused of running a 'house of ill repute' as the Sunday papers would doubtlessly describe it."

"OK, I can understand that. Now, this Tim, you have a name for him? And an address perhaps?"

"Of course, I have. This is a members-only club and membership cards obviously include the full name and address, etc. Although whether I should reveal that to you or not is another matter, customer confidentiality and all that you know."

Manners looked at him coldly. "I would advise you not to piss me about too much Jonny, old son, this is a murder investigation and you have already stretched my patience about as far as it will go. So, you either answer my questions here or we will continue this conversation at the station where we will also discuss a charge of obstructing the course of justice. So, it might well be in your interest to co-operate as much as you can. Do you understand me?"

"Christ! You didn't say anything about murder! Who has been killed?"

"Never mind that, just answer my questions and no more pissing about, right?"

"Yeah, of course, sorry."

"So, what about this Tim, then, is he in here this evening?"

"Not yet, he usually comes in about eight or so."

"Every night?"

"No, not on Mondays or Sundays and hardly ever on a Saturday."

"Right, I want his name and address and a description of him."

"I can do better than that, I can give you a photograph of him."

"A photo? Surely you don't put their picture on their membership card?"

"No, of course not, but I do have a picture of all our members. They don't know that, so I would be obliged if you didn't broadcast the fact."

"And just how do you do that then?"

"When someone comes in and wishes to become a member, they give the doorman fifty pounds. They would then be directed in to see me at the gin rack, that's the part of the bar in front of the gin optics of course. They fill in an application form and I turn up the lights over that area so they can see what they are doing and take a digital picture of them."

"With one of those mini cameras that look almost like optics on the two bottles of Japanese gin, I take it?"

"Oh, are they that obvious, Sergeant?"

"Probably not to your average punter, no, but we law enforcement chaps do tend to be a little more observant than your average punter. But what happens if someone wants a shot of the Japanese gin?"

"That's never happened yet, but if it did, we have another bottle on the shelf just behind the optic. So, all those images are stored on my computer here and they are renewed annually with their membership."

"And the fifty pounds to the doorman?"

"They pay me forty pounds for the membership then, when they leave, they show the doorman their membership card and he gives them back their fifty. We look upon it as a sort of deposit, pending their acceptance. Of course, I suspect that sometimes they might be inclined to leave some of it with the doorman, as a token of gratitude, you might say, but that has nothing to do with me."

"And how many members do you have?"

"About two hundred and thirty some odd – I can check the exact number if you want?"

"No, that won't be necessary."

He turned the computer monitor so that they could both see the screen, and said, "Now, let's see if we can find Tim for you," He tapped on the keyboard and an array of thumbnail images appeared which he scrolled through, then said, "Ah, here he is, Timothy Vernon." He pressed another key and the screen filled with a full-face image of a clean-shaven man in his early thirties. "Would you like me to print a hard copy of that for you?"

"Yes, I would, and what is his address?"

"Well, I have an address for him here in Kings Dalton, but I can't guarantee it. Some members have been known to be rather economical with the truth when it comes to divulging their address and, of course, we have no way, nor desire for that matter, to verify them." He reached behind him to a printer which sat on a filing cabinet and removed a large, coloured print of Vernon. He wrote an address on the back and handed it to Manners.

On a sudden whim, Manners took two more photographs from his pocket and laid them on the desk. "Do you recognise either of these two gentlemen?" he asked.

Jonny peered at them, then tapped the picture of Denton. "He's a member. Often comes in with Colin but not as frequently and they don't usually sit together."

"And is he a 'friend' of Tim?"

"Probably, most members are."

"Do you know his name?"

"Not off-hand but I could look it up."

"Try Harry Denton, then."

Jonny tapped away at his keyboard for a few moments and a picture of Denton appeared on the screen. "Yes, Harry Denton, been a member for about six years but, as I say, not so frequent as Colin."

"And the other one?"

He looked at the picture of Peters and shuddered. "Heavens, no! He would never get past Wayne looking like that."

"Wayne?"

"The doorman. Or Barry, his relief."

"Thank you, and what is your name?"

"Alistair Fairburn."

"Jonny?"

"Well, Alistair Jon Fairburn, but I have always been known as Jonny, and that suits me here."

"And you are the Landlord and proprietor here?"

"Good Lord, no! I am the registered landlord, but the club and the premises are owned by a consortium from Birmingham. They have another four clubs besides this one, and as long as the money keeps rolling in, they don't worry me over much. I am left to run the place pretty much as I will."

"Well, thank you, Jonny, that will be all for the moment, but we will need a statement from you. You can call into the station to provide that, preferably within the next forty-eight hours."

"Will that be necessary?"

"Yes, it certainly will."

Jonny looked up above Manners' head. "Just a moment, it looks as if Tim has just come in."

Manners twisted round in his chair and saw a row of four monitors mounted on the wall above the door obviously connected to CCTV cameras mounted in strategic positions throughout the club. One of them appeared to be permanently fixed on the entrance and the others cycled between the bar, the dancefloor and various other points. He saw a short-ish man walking towards the bar, and as he got closer, he recognised him from the photograph as Tim Vernon.

"Bring him in here then before he settles down, and I'll speak to him here."

Jonny shrugged and left the room. Manners watched on the monitors, and he saw him approach Vernon. They had a short conversation, then Jonny put a hand firmly on his shoulder and guided him towards the bar. They disappeared from the monitor and then the door opened, and Jonny ushered him in. "Thank you," said Manners, "You can leave us now, I'll let you know when we've finished."

Jonny looked about to protest but then shrugged again and closed the door, appearing shortly afterwards on the monitor whose camera was trained on the centre of the bar.

Manners indicated to the other chair in front of the desk and said, "You are Timothy Vernon?"

"Yes, what's this all about?"

"Sit there. I am Detective Sergeant Manners of County CID and I want to ask you a few questions. Before I start, though, I think that I should tell you that I am not in the best of moods; I have been pissed about tonight to just about the limit of my tolerance, so if you get any ideas along those lines forget them. We can just as easily conduct this interview at the station, under caution. Do you understand that?"

"Christ, I haven't said a word, yet, but yes, Sergeant, I do understand, and I can assure you that I have no intention of pissing anyone around, as you put it."

"Good. Now, do you know Colin Jacques?"

"Yes, of course, we are friends."

"And where were you on the evening of Tuesday the twenty-second of this month, between seven p.m. and ten p.m.?"

"Tuesday? Then I would have been in here."

"Are you sure?"

"I am here almost every Tuesday and, if I wasn't it would have been unusual enough for me to remember. So, yes, I am sure."

"And can anyone vouch for that?"

"Well, Jonny, he never misses anything, possibly the doorman, although I wouldn't like to rely on his memory, and Colin, of course. Colin and I were here together all evening at least from about eight when he usually comes in."

"Until ten?"

"Oh, yes."

"And then?"

"May I be permitted to ask what this about?"

"Yes, this is a murder enquiry and I'm asking the questions."

"Murder? Not Colin?"

"Colin isn't dead as far as I know, no. Now, you were about to tell me where you and Colin were after ten p.m. on that Tuesday, remember?"

Vernon gulped. "We went back to Colin's place for a coffee and nightcap as we usually do."

"Usually? On Tuesdays?"

"Yes, and Fridays."

"And what time did you leave there?"

"Um, er."

"Don't be coy, Mr. Vernon, it doesn't become you."

He sighed. "I left Colin's house at about seven the next

morning, as I usually do. Satisfied?"

"And are you prepared to give evidence to that effect in court?"

Vernon gulped again and wiped his damp forehead with a handkerchief. "If it was necessary, I suppose so, yes."

"And how well do you know Harry Denton? I believe he too is a friend of yours."

"I know Harry, of course, but I wouldn't really class him as a friend. More an acquaintance perhaps?"

"Would that be an intimate acquaintance?"

"On occasion, but he isn't really my sort."

"Thank you, Mr. Vernon, that will be all for now. We may need to question you again, so please don't leave the area without informing us. And we will need a formal statement from you covering what you have told me this evening, so I would be obliged if you would call into the County Police Headquarters tomorrow morning between nine a.m. and twelve when we can arrange for that to be taken, together with your fingerprints and a DNA sample, if you have no objections."

"Fingerprints and DNA?"

"Purely for elimination purposes. So, I need keep you no longer, Mr. Vernon, please be good enough to ask Jonny to step back in here if you would."

When Jonny came back into the office, Manners said, "I think that's all for now. As I said, we will need a statement from you to the effect that both Colin Jacques and Timothy Vernon were here between the hours that we discussed and, naturally, we would expect you to co-operate with that, right?"

"Of course, Sergeant. May I offer you a drink before you go?"

"No, thank you, I believe in paying for my own drinks and I

don't think a Sergeant's pay would run to one of your concoctions."

"A whisky, perhaps?"

"No, thank you, I will be off." Manners walked out of the club, ignoring the doorman and got back into his car with an enormous sigh of relief.

As he pulled onto his drive, Jean opened the door for him. "Hello, stranger, do I know you?"

"Hello gorgeous, am I glad to see a normal human person!"

"Oh, you say the sweetest things, you charmer you."

"God, honey I am in desperate need of a shower, a very large glass of something special and a cuddle."

"In that order?"

"Certainly not! The shower could possibly wait for a moment or two, but the cuddle definitely can't."

She put her arms round his neck and kissed him. "Want to talk about it?"

"Not in detail, no, but I have just spent an hour in the New Moon gay club and if anyone, up to and including the Home Secretary ever asks me to go there again I shall shoot myself or more likely, them!"

"Oh, that bad, was it?"

"No, honey, it was much worse than that. In hindsight, I wish I had sent Pete, but I fear there might have been a blood bath if I had. You know he doesn't have my lovely gift of tender tolerance and patience."

"Lovely gift of tender tolerance and patience? You? Well, well. I learn something new every day!"

"Don't push your luck, sweetie, you're far too young to die."

"Go and shower yourself, then, husband dear, and we can discuss this in a more civilised manner over a glass or two of something damp."

"OK, but just before I do that, come here." He kissed her again and she pushed him onto the sofa. "Yes, oh, Master, was there something?" She gently pulled down his zip and slid her hand into his boxer shorts.

"Jean Manners! What on earth are you doing?" he mumbled.

"I'll give you three guesses."

"Um, I think one will be enough."

Thirty-Four

At precisely eight a.m., DCI Parker entered the incident room and called for attention. "Right, we have a lot to get through this morning, so let's get on with it. Just to bring you all up-to-date, Colin Jacques was interviewed again yesterday by Sergeant Manners and myself. He provided an alibi for the night that Denton was killed, he claimed that he was with a 'friend' from the New Moon gay club from about eight p.m. until seven the following morning. Dave was rather busy yesterday evening trying to verify that alibi and will report on his adventure shortly but, from Jacques' reluctance to admit to that sort of relationship, I suspect that it might be true. His alibi for the twenty-fifth, when Peters was killed, is impossible to verify but rings true. Now, that means that if, and I stress the 'if', he is telling the truth, then someone deliberately planted the evidence of the hair dye, contact lenses, ID card and cable ties on him."

"But Sunni said you have evidence that Jacques bought the cable ties from Screwbase, Guv," called Corbett.

"Not exactly, Ronnie, no. We have evidence that someone calling himself Colin Jacques and giving his address, bought them," said Sunni, "but, he was served by the manager of the local branch, and when I asked if she would recognise him she said that they average well over a hundred sales a day and unless he looked like Tom Cruise or George Clooney she would be unlikely to!"

Parker continued. "Meanwhile, I was obliged to release him

yesterday as his twenty-four hours was up with regard to the mugging, and I didn't think we had enough evidence to seek an extension."

There were groans, but he held up his hand and said, "However, as he left, young DC Patel here promptly re-arrested him, and he has been charged with possession with intent and will appear at Elmington Magistrates Court tomorrow morning. As you will know, the minimum sentence, if convicted, is seven years, but, with his record he could be facing anything up to life."

There were cheers and calls of 'Yes!' as hands punched the air in delight and relief.

Sunni stood up and said, "And I have some even more good cheer there, Guv. As you suggested, I handed his record book, which we found in his cache of cash, to the drugs squad and, apart from Zack Peters, they have been able to identify, or perhaps guess at, another seven of his buyers who they are talking to even as we speak! And would you believe it, my friends, but three of those were identified because our master criminal had written their phone numbers down alongside their initials."

There was general laughter and calls of disbelief. "You're joking!"

"Pull the other one."

"What a pillock!"

"Sergeant Manners had also suggested," continued Patel, "that they compare the list of initials with the membership records at the New Moon, and although I get the impression that they pretend not to welcome tips from lowly souls like us, I believe they intend to follow that up."

"That's excellent, Sunni, well done to them," said Parker. "Now Phil, anything on Peters' passport?"

"Yes, Guv, eventually I was able to speak to a real live

person at Newport passport office, and he confirmed that there has never been a passport issued to a Cecil John Peters or even to a Zachary Peters for that matter."

"Thanks. Now, Beryl, what about friend Jacques? You were looking into his background and finances."

"As far as his background is concerned, we know about his record and his drugs dealings of course and there is no doubt at all about his sexual predilections, so him frequenting the New Moon club would be a given. His finances, though, are much more complicated. We are talking about hundreds of thousands of pounds, here, and, quite frankly, Guv, that's way beyond my expertise. I passed it all over to Bernard Fellowes, our forensic accountant, but he says that it will take weeks to sort out, but at first glance he has no doubt that, in his words, 'it reeks of laundry'. I hope it was OK to do that, Guv?"

"Yes, of course, Beryl, no question at all."

Thirty-Five

He looked at Lee. "Pete, did you get to see Richard Fleming?"

"Oh yes, Guv, in fact I got two for the price of one! His son, Tony, was with him when I called, keeping an eye on the old chap, I think. And I believe that he is absolutely genuine, although I couldn't get much out of him; the death of his wife has left him totally devastated. Even the simplest question I asked him merely resulted in a shake of the head, in fact I don't think he even heard me half the time. He agreed to being fingerprinted and swabbed for DNA, although whether he really understood what that was all about is anybody's guess. And there was no trace of the humour he showed when Dave and I interviewed him before."

"You mean the reference to the small..."

"Yes, yes. No need to labour that. *Sir*."

"Sorry, Pete, but we did think that was a rather amusing description."

Lee rolled his eyes and continued. "I was impressed with his son, a real chip off the old block. Neither of them showed anything other than quiet satisfaction when I told them that both Denton and Peters were dead. Tony asked how they had died, and I merely said that they been killed, neither asked how or when and Richard showed no signs of realising the implications of that, but Tony said something to the effect that he owed the killer his heart-felt gratitude, and that he would happily have done it himself but wouldn't have known who to shoot! So, all in all, Sir,

I think that I spent about an hour or so with two very decent, heart-broken men and I would like to suggest that we now leave them alone in their grief."

"Thank you, Peter, that's excellent, and I am happy to go along with that, unless anything crops up to change that opinion of course."

"Thanks, Guv, but I would be very surprised if it does."

Thirty-Six

Parker turned to PC Carter. "Now, George, I understand that you had an interesting time tracing our pharmacist, didn't you?"

"I did indeed, Guv."

"Well, come up here and tell all."

George made his way to the front of the room and stood next to Parker. "You will recall, perhaps, that I noted a visit to Bolton Ward of a pharmacist on the morning of Tuesday the twenty-second. A normal and by no means unusual routine, by all accounts. I had recorded him as Roger Newman, BPharm, apparently from the hospital pharmacy, and a very pleasant character he seemed, too. However, when I visited the pharmacy, the boss lady there agreed that they do, certainly, visit all the wards as a matter of course, to ensure that they have sufficient medication in stock to meet the prescribed requirements of all the current patients. But, gentleman, oh and er, lady, she had no knowledge of a Roger Newman. 'Never heard of him,' she said, and I noticed that her identity badge was nothing like the one sported by the so-called Roger Newman. So, as our Guvnor had suggested, that this could have been a ruse to identify an admission with a leg wound, and as I recalled that the 'pharmacist' had used what I thought was a mobile phone, presumably with a camera, when he was in with Denton, I investigated further.

"I honestly wasn't sure where to start, so I contacted the hospital switchboard operators to see if anyone could remember any enquiries that, with hindsight, might appear to be suspicious. The third operator that I spoke to remembered such a call. She wasn't sure which day it had been, but she remembered it because they had been alerted to the fact that the details of Denton's admission should not be disclosed. The call was from a firm of private investigators who were trying to trace a missing person. She said that she merely confirmed that a person with a leg injury had been seen in A&E but gave no more details than that. At first she could not recall the name of the firm, but when I suggested a few, she thought that Hampton and Gillis rang a bell. That rang a bell with me, too. I had served with Bert Hampton in the Gloucestershire force, and I remember that he took early retirement, under something of a cloud. There had been some talk of bribes when he was on vice, but nothing was ever proven and, as I say, he retired early and set up a private investigation and security business with Frank Gillis, of whom I knew nothing. Bert was a large, burly chap and nothing at all like the pharmacist, and of course I would have recognised him if had been him, but I decided to pay them a visit anyway. When I entered their office in Elmington, Bingo! I came face to face with one Roger Newman BPharm AKA Frank Gillis, and to his utter dismay, he recognised me too."

He took a sip from a bottle of water and continued. "We had a most interesting chat. At first, he argued that it wasn't an offence to impersonate a pharmacist; he said that he had checked and the only instance he could find of someone being charged with that was in America and that was because it involved not only the impersonation, but also the dispensing of drugs etc. So, he thought that although it was perhaps not totally ethical, it was not illegal. I must confess, Sir, that I wasn't too sure about it myself, but I invited him to tell me the whole story or I would arrest him, if not for impersonating a pharmacist, then for at least seven other offences, none of which I could think of at the time, but I told him that they would certainly include conspiracy to commit murder." He grinned. "I thought he was going to mess himself, but he suddenly became all too keen to tell me everything that he could remember.

"He said that the whole charade was at the behest, and suggestion, of a so-say 'client' of his who said that he was anxious to trace the whereabouts of his nephew, and thought it possible that he had been injured and hence admitted to hospital, but under a false name. Gillis admitted that he had taken a photograph of Denton and of the ID sticker on his hospital notes, but was secretly pleased when Mr. Thompson, his client, disclaimed all knowledge of him and assured Gillis that it was definitely not his nephew. His description of 'Alan Thompson', as he introduced himself, bore little resemblance to the Sinclair impostor other than his height, although, as I've already said, I would be hard pressed to recognise him anyway. This Alan Thompson, if that was his real name, was perhaps a couple of inches shorter than me, so Gillis said, which would make him a little over five-ten, but he was quite thin and had short grey hair.

"Gillis, unsurprisingly, had no record of this escapade on his books, so I assume that the 'fee' went straight into his pocket. I got the impression, Guv, that, after he had convinced himself that it was not actually illegal, he looked upon it as a bit of excitement to liven his, I suspect, rather dull everyday routine. And doubtlessly profitable too. He will be coming in at nine a.m. tomorrow morning to make a formal statement, Sir, and, oh yes, I confiscated his passport."

"You confiscated his passport? What on earth for?"

"Just to give him something to worry about, Sir, I felt it was the least I could do!"

"Oh, I like your style George, *but…*"

"Yes, of course, Guv. There was one other thing, though." He pulled a small transparent evidence bag from his pocket with something of a flourish. "I have here the false ID tag that he said Alan Thompson had given him and, fortuitously, or perhaps stupidly, had forgotten to ask for back."

"Well, that is good, George, you've played a blinder there. Remind me to buy you a pint sometime."

There were ribald calls from all round the room. "And if you believe that, George, me boy, you'll believe anything!"

"Well, there's a first time for everything, they say."

"Even so, but the Guvnor actually buying a drink? That's pure fantasy."

"All right, all right, children," said Parker with a grin, "cut it out. Let's get back to business."

Thirty-Seven

DCI Parker looked at Corbett. "Ronnie? What of our Mr. Mason?"

"Yes, Guv, I went to see Mason, but, bearing in mind what Pete had said about the Elmington Players, I thought I would drop into the Playhouse on the off-chance that I might learn something of interest, and it was on my way to Kings Dalton any way. And in the event, I'm glad I did. I spoke to Pete before we left last night and, digging into his world-famous memory, he thought that Elizabeth Fellows was the Producer/Director named on the 'Pirates of Penzance' poster. He was wrong, of course! It was Elizabeth Farrow, but close enough I suppose!"

He grinned at Lee, then continued. "By a stroke of luck, Elizabeth was in the Playhouse when I got there; they had a rehearsal that evening, but she was in the wardrobe department checking on the outfits and props for their next production which is only two weeks away. The 'Gondoliers' apparently, Peter. She was most helpful. She said that Arthur Mason is a long-time member of the 'Players'; he had once tried his luck at acting, at his wife's insistence but was, as he would readily admit she said, a total disaster. He can neither act nor sing she said, but is a genius with the sound and lights so that has been his forte ever since his acting debut.

"I noticed when I went in that she was holding what I took to be a white jumper of some sort, but she was looking puzzled. 'A problem?' I asked, more to be friendly than out of any real interest. She said, 'No, I have just found this and have never seen it before, but wondered if we could use it to pad out Reg for his Duke of Plaza-Toro in the Gondoliers.' It was an inflatable 'body-enhancer' of all things, Guv, and I remembered George saying that Sinclair was stockily built but all our suspects weren't, apart from Jacques, of course, so I wondered. She was adamant that it hadn't been in the wardrobe department long, and had no idea where it had come from – 'some benefactor', she supposed. I asked if there was anything else in there that was new or unusual, but she was sure there wasn't. I then asked about their make-up department, was there anything untoward or missing, but again she was sure that there wasn't. I asked about contact lenses, and she said they would be of little use in a stage production, but she remembered they had produced a video version of 'Cats' about a year ago, and although she wasn't personally involved with that, she knew that most of the girls wore coloured lenses, but they were all green, naturally. She checked for me and confirmed that there were none missing.

"Then, we got back to the Pirates and Arthur's wife, Louise. Well, there Guv, I think we jumped to a conclusion; when he said that he had lost her, it was assumed he meant that she had died."

"True," said Pete, "but?"

"But she isn't dead. And this is where that poster of the show some years ago has real significance. She was due to sing the role of Mabel, one of the leading characters apparently. But when she and Arthur got home after the dress rehearsal on the night before the opening, they opened their front door and disturbed two burglars who had broken in through the patio doors at the back. In the confrontation that ensued, Louise was hit viciously in the head with, ironically, Arthur's favourite figurine. It was a marble replica of the Venus de Milo that Louise had bought him for their

Ruby Wedding Anniversary the previous year. And shades of the Harpers Lane mugging gentlemen, she was admitted to hospital with a severely fractured skull. Unlike Mary Fleming, though, she survived, but after some weeks in an induced coma she developed Alzheimer's and has been in the Nightingale Nursing Home here in Elmington ever since.

"I visited them and spoke to the Manager. She said that Arthur used to visit his wife twice a day as regular as clockwork when she was first admitted, but her condition rapidly worsened and his visits, understandably, became less frequent. After a few months she could not recognise him and she grew increasingly violent, towards him and her carers. He was devastated, naturally, and now visits just once or twice a week 'more in hope than in expectation' as he puts it. So, before I went to see him, I checked if the incident involving the burglary had been recorded and, of course, it had been. The Investigating Officer was Inspector Chalmers, whom most of us remember and who retired last year. I took the liberty of phoning him Sir, and he confirmed what Ms. Farrow had told me. There had been no arrests relating to the incident, there were no fingerprints on anything, and the only witness was a rather elderly neighbour who thought she had seen two men clambering over her back garden fence that night. Her descriptions were not much help, said Inspector Chalmers, except that I noted that she thought that one of them had a ponytail 'flapping behind him as he ran' as she had put it. Now I'm sure that Peters isn't the only thieving berk around here with a ponytail but, who knows?

"So, in the light of that, Guv, as you know, I returned here and explained to you that I thought that I should be accompanied on my visit to him, and Beryl Watson joined me. Neither Beryl nor I had seen him before, so we introduced ourselves and he invited us in with no hesitation. I explained that we had a few more questions that we would like to ask him, and he readily agreed, though he reiterated that he thought he had already given us all the information that he could. I asked him about the poster for 'The Pirates of Penzance' and he confirmed what Elizabeth had told me. His wife should have been singing the role of Mabel, and that poster represented, to him, the last time that he and Louise had, as he put it, enjoyed a normal life together. He was naturally deeply distressed about the whole affair, so I didn't push it. When I asked what other interests he had, he told us that he played Skittles for the Red Lion once a week, he was an Honorary Life Member of the Elmington Photographic Society, belonged to the local Philatelic Group and was a keen cyclist. We took his fingerprints and a DNA swab and left him to it."

"OK," said Parker, "I believe you wanted to add a thought, Dave?"

"Yes. After my jolly sojourn in the New Moon Club last night, I think that the 'open mind' that we are all keeping should include the possibility of a gay scenario. Not only was Jacques a long time and very active member of that club but so, to a somewhat lesser degree, was our Harry Denton. It could perhaps be the result of homophobia, 'queer bashing' I think was the old non-P.C. term and there's a lot of that about it seems, even I, would you believe, have been accused of being homophobic twice in as many days. Or it could be jealousy within the gay community, and I suspect that that community is considerably larger and more widespread than many of us had imagined. I have no evidence of either, but I intend to dig a little deeper into Mr. Timothy Vernon and also Alistair Jon Fairburn, landlord of the Moon, just to rattle their cages and see what happens."

"OK, Dave, thanks for that. It is certainly an angle that hadn't occurred to us before. So, that about wraps it up for today, you all know what you have to do, so get on with it. Is there anything else for now?"

"Yes, Guv," interjected Lee, "it's Mary Fleming's funeral tomorrow, and Dave and I would like to attend, if you have no objections. Dave will be in Court for Jacques' hearing in the morning, but the funeral isn't until one o'clock, so he should be well clear by then."

"Of course, Pete, I have no objection to that at all. If you get a chance to speak to Richard, give him my condolences."

"Thanks, and we'll do that."

"Right, next briefing same time tomorrow, and I'm hoping that by then we might have heard something back from forensics, they seem to be dragging their heels a bit."

Thirty-Eight

The briefing meeting the next morning was short. DCI Parker reported that forensics had confirmed that there were no fingerprints on any of the items recovered from the refuse bins at Jacques' property. The contact lenses had been the most likely items to contain traces of DNA, but they had apparently been washed thoroughly before being refitted into their case. But the pieces of fake ID card were identical in a number of ways to the card purporting to belong to a Roger Newman BPharm that George Carter had recovered from Frank Gillis. They had been printed on identical photo paper using identical ink and were glued to pieces of identical card with identical adhesive. Apart from a number of prints identified as belonging to Frank Gillis, there was a partial print on the latter card which they had identified, albeit without the one hundred percent certainty they would have liked, but enough to warrant a confrontation with the suspect, if desired.

Later in the morning, Dave Manners knocked on Parker's door. "Great news, Guv, Jacques has been remanded in custody pending his appearance at Gloucester Crown Court at a date yet to be set for next month."

***

The tiny parish church of St Mary in Kings Dalton was packed for the funeral of Mary Fleming. Manners and Lee had edged their way in and stood at the back as the organ was playing gently in the background. Suddenly, the music changed to a recording of 'Wind beneath my Wings' as the coffin was carried in and placed on two trestles at the front of the aisle. Richard was supported by his son, Tony, as they followed the coffin, and behind them was Tony's wife Sally and a man and woman, both in their thirties whom Manners assumed, rightly, to be the twin grandchildren that Richards had spoken of with such pride.

The Vicar who conducted the service had obviously known Mary and spoke of her movingly. After the first hymn he called on Lucy, the granddaughter, to read the tribute that she had prepared; she stood at the front with her brother, he holding her hand, and with tears flowing freely down her face, gave the most loving and emotional eulogy to her Gran that Manners had ever heard. He stole a quick glance at the huge man standing next to him and saw a single tear running down his cheek. *'You great softie',* he thought but the lump in his throat would have prevented him from saying it out loud.

As the service ended, a recording of Andrea Bocelli singing 'Time to say Goodbye' brought tears to many more eyes as the congregation slowly filed out, shaking hands with the family and sharing a few words with them. Dave and Pete commiserated sincerely with Richard who seemed surprised, but pleased, to see them. He spoke with difficulty but thanked them for coming and his handshake was remarkably firm. They both praised his granddaughter for her eulogy and quietly moved away.

As they had stood at the back of the church, Lee had noticed that Arthur Mason was sitting in one of the pews a few rows behind Richard and nodded in approval. As Mason left, having spoken to the family, he made his way to the Lychgate deep in thought but suddenly found his way blocked by two figures. He looked up and recognised DC Corbett. "Arthur Mason, I am Detective Constable Corbett."

"Yes, I know."

"And this is Detective Chief Inspector Parker. I am arresting you on suspicion of murder. You do not have to say anything. But it may harm your defence if you do not mention when questioned something which you later rely on in court. Anything you do say may be given in evidence. Do you understand that?"

Mason looked surprised for a moment, then resigned. "Yes, of course, I understand."

"I would like you to accompany us to the station where, if you wish, a legal representative will be made available to you."

"That won't be necessary. May I take my car? It will probably be in the way of the next service as it is on the road just outside the Lychgate."

Corbett looked at Parker who nodded. "OK, I will come with you. You can take the car to your home then I will arrange for a car to take us to the station."

Thirty-Nine

Back at the station, Mason had been 'processed' by the Custody Sergeant, emptied his pockets and was asked to remove his tie, belt and shoelaces. "Is that really necessary?" he asked.

"Purely routine, Sir, I'm afraid."

He was asked again if he wished to be represented and, on advice from DCI Parker, changed his mind and agreed to accept the duty solicitor. He was led away to a cell and was told that he would be held there until the solicitor arrived when they would be allowed as much time together for private discussion as required.

Simon Trenchard was a young but highly capable partner in a firm of local Solicitors. Parker had known him for some years and, although they had sometimes crossed swords in court, and not always to Parker's advantage, he had to admit that he had great respect for him and was pleased that he was the duty solicitor. 'Mason could do no better,' he thought.

When Trenchard arrived at the station, he was shown into Parker's office and offered the inevitable coffee. "No, thank you, Chief Inspector, I'm too young to die."

Parker grinned and passed him a folder with Mason's name on the top and a photograph clipped to the front cover. "Your client, Simon, is a Mr. Arthur Mason. He has been arrested on suspicion of murder but has not yet been charged, of course. When arrested he made no comment other than he thought legal representation would not be necessary. However, I advised him that it would be in his best interest if he were, and he agreed. At the moment is he in our custody and you, of course, may have as much time with him privately as you wish."

"Thank you, Chief Inspector, now may I ask what evidence you have to support the allegation?"

"Certainly, it's all in the folder there, but I would be happy to go over it with you."

Trenchard picked up the folder and said, "Would you allow me a few minutes?"

"By all means."

Simon opened the folder and scanned swiftly through the contents. "Can you give me some background on him? As much as you can, please."

Parker leant back in his chair and told Trenchard as much as he could about Mason. He repeated everything that DC Corbett had reported and said that forensics were 'pretty sure' that it was his fingerprint on the fake ID card that Gillis had used to impersonate a hospital pharmacist and gain access to Denton's room. It was not their usual 'one hundred percent certainty' but they felt it would be enough for an identity, particularly if supported by other evidence. He stressed that the pieces of fake ID card found in Jacques' bin were, in forensics' opinion, identical to Gillis' card so felt it highly unlikely that Mason could deny it was he who had hired Gillis, especially as Gillis was certain that he would be able to pick out 'Alan Thompson' from an identity line-up if necessary.

"So, you think that my client was this 'Mr. Sinclair' who visited Harry Denton in Bolton Ward?"

"We are reasonably sure, yes."

"Evidence?"

"Other than the fake ID card you mean? Well, an inflatable

body enhancer was found in the wardrobe department of the Playhouse Theatre, to which Mr. Mason has free and ample access. And it may well have been such a device that was worn by whoever passed himself off as Sinclair and, other than his bulk, or lack of it, he could, with a little hair dye and a phoney Scottish burr well have been Mason."

"May? Chief Inspector? May? And could he be positively identified as Sinclair by your Constable who allowed him access to Denton's room? Or by the nurse who offered to accompany him into the room but whose offer was declined?"

"Unlikely that they could, positively, Simon, I must agree. And he was, of course, wearing a face mask."

"So circumstantial at best then?"

"The fake ID card isn't circumstantial."

"Quite so, but there seems to be little else, hmm? Unless you are hoping for a confession of course. Now, what evidence do you have to link him to this Peters chap?" He glanced at the notes in the folder. "Cecil John Peters, AKA 'Zack', I see."

"A packet of plastic cable ties, identical to those that were used to garrotte Mr. Peters was found in Colin Jacques' van at the same time as the pieces of fake ID card, hair dye and contact lenses were found in his rubbish bin. There were no fingerprints or DNA, but if Mason had planted the card, etc. then..."

"Oh, come on, Chief Inspector, that is pure assumption. If, and I stress the 'if', Mr. Mason had planted the pieces of card in Jacques' bin, how can you *assume* that he must therefore have planted some cable ties in a totally different location and *assume* that they were planted at the same time? The fact that you discovered them at the same time is merely because that was when you conducted your search of his premises and is certainly no reason for you to *assume* that they were put there at the same time, or by the same person. Do you have any evidence to connect my client to these cable ties? Do you have any evidence, or witnesses, to place my client anywhere near the motorcycle on which the unfortunate Cecil Peters met his death? Indeed, do you have any evidence whatsoever to link my client with Cecil Peters at all? I think, Chief Inspector, that you are making a lot of unsubstantiated assumptions here; you are assuming that my client impersonated a doctor in order to gain access to Harry Denton. You are assuming that Mr. Denton then told him the names and addresses of two people, whom you assume were his accomplices in a mugging which, you assume, Mr. Denton carried out. And above all, you assume that my client would *want* to kill, or seek revenge on, three men of whom he had caught only the merest fleeting glimpse as he stopped to help two elderly people who were being assaulted. Really, Chief Inspector, I think you might save us all a lot of time and expense if you let Mr. Mason go home now, with an apology for worrying him."

DCI Parker clapped his hands slowly and nodded. "Bravo, Simon, well done, that was very impressive. But you know of course that isn't how it's done. We will interview Mr. Mason, he is already under caution, and hear what he has to say, if he can explain away all the *circumstantial* evidence that we have and, indeed, if he has an alibi for any of the times that these events took place. Please avail yourself of his company now and D.C. Corbett, as the arresting officer, and I will join you in the interview room whenever you are ready."

Simon gathered the papers into his folder and held out his hand. "Thank you Reg, I will do that."

Forty

As a courtesy to Simon, Parker had arranged for him to use the interview room rather than the cell in which to conduct his discussion with Mason. "Good afternoon, Mr Mason, my name is Simon Trenchard, and I am the solicitor appointed to represent you in this unfortunate matter, if you have no objections?"

"No, of course not."

"Good, then, in that case, before we start, I would like to make one important thing clear to you. You will doubtlessly have heard many of the old music hall jokes about lawyers, with the inference that we are not always as honest as we might seem? In fact, I understand that there are one or two pubs called 'The Honest Lawyer' as though they are a rarity. Well, I want to assure you that that is most decidedly not the case. The vast majority of my profession are decent, honest and hard-working men and women."

"I'm sure you are right."

"But my point is, Mr. Mason, that I, and any Barrister who may represent you in court, should it come to that, may not, and indeed will not, say anything in court that we know, or believe, to be untrue. So, if, for example, you were to tell me that you had killed x, y or z, then we could not tell the court that you had not killed x, y or z. All we could do would be to present any mitigating evidence, or argue that the killing was perhaps accidental, or at the very least was not premeditated. Because a premeditated killing is a very serious business, Mr. Mason, and almost always results in a sentence of life imprisonment. You understand what I am saying?"

"Yes, of course I do."

"So be very careful what you say to me, please don't lie to me, and it would be best if you just answer my questions and, whatever you do, don't volunteer any information to our friendly, neighbourhood policemen who will be interviewing you as soon as we have finished our chat here. Right?"

"Yes, whatever you say, Sir, but I am quite prepared to admit to anything that I have done, and to face any consequences."

"That's very laudable, Mr. Mason, but I think that our Chief Inspector had visions of charging you with at least one, and possibly two, murders and if you were to, let us say confess to those, then a life sentence would follow as sure as night follows day. So please, be guided by me."

"Thank you, I will do as you say."

"Good. Now, from the evidence that Mr. Parker has, it seems that they can prove, beyond reasonable doubt, that you employed a Mr. Frank Gillis, of Hampton and Gillis, private investigators, to impersonate a hospital pharmacist with the intention of establishing the identity and whereabouts of the person who was suspected of the assault on Mr. and Mrs. Fleming on the night of Tuesday the fifteenth. An assault that was interrupted by your timely intervention, but from which Mrs. Fleming later sadly died."

"Well, I... "

Trenchard held up his hand. "A moment, please, hear me out."

"Sorry."

"If you feel that Mr. Gillis could indeed positively identify you as the 'Mr. Alan Thompson' who employed him and who provided him with the fake ID card, then there would be no point in you denying it, indeed, doing so would make you appear to be a liar and that would do our future arguments no good at all."

"Yes, of course, I will freely admit that it was me. I posed as Alan Thompson, a name that I picked out of thin air, and it was my idea that Frank Gillis should pose as a hospital pharmacist as you have suggested."

"Thank you, but that, then, may well suggest that, because of the similarities of the fake ID cards that were used, it was you who impersonated a doctor in order to gain access to Mr. Denton in Bolton Ward and who, as I'm sure the good Chief Inspector will allege, subsequently caused his death."

"Yes, I see that."

"But why on earth would you do that? It could be, one might suppose, in order to exact revenge – but he had done you no wrong. Or perhaps, it was in order to extract from him the identities of his accomplices, always assuming of course that Mr. Denton had been one of the attackers involved, an assumption which, of course, had not been, and could not now be, proven. But, if this latter were the case, then any subsequent incidents involving either of his two, shall we say accomplices, would naturally infer premeditation, a term which we would wish to avoid at all costs."

Mason nodded his head but said nothing.

"There is, though," continued Trenchard, "a third possibility that occurs to me, and I have to be very careful here not to put words into your mouth, but it is conceivable that the intention of identifying the other two participants in the assault was solely to assist the police with their enquiries."

"Then why wasn't that information passed to them sooner?"

"Possibly it was thought that passing that information too

quickly might leave the 'passer' liable to be accused of being the imposter who, however unintentionally, had caused Denton's death."

"So, you think Denton's death was unintentional then?"

"Well, if Mr. Sinclair had in fact been Colin Jacques, as the circumstantial evidence found in his rubbish bin seemed to suggest, then, no, it would be seen as a deliberate act to prevent him from identifying Jacques as one of the attackers. However, as Colin Jacques appears to have a fairly substantial alibi, then we must assume that Mr. Denton's death was indeed unintentional, an unfortunate accident in fact.

"Now, Mr. Mason, let me ask you a couple of questions, and please just answer yes or no."

"Go ahead."

"Did you impersonate a doctor in order to gain access to Mr. Denton?"

"No."

"No?"

"Well, not exactly. I didn't actually tell anybody that I was a doctor. I said that I was Alec Sinclair, but when the Constable on Denton's door called me 'doctor' I told him that I was 'mister' not 'doctor'."

"But because surgeons are called 'mister' and physicians are 'doctor', right?"

"Well, yes."

"And you know that Alec Sinclair, whose identity you had assumed, was a surgeon, did you not?"

"Yes."

"Then you impersonated a doctor, Mr. Mason, so please don't split hairs."

"I'm sorry, I was just trying to be as factual as I could. I had no intention to mislead you."

"OK, but I have to tell you that splitting hairs like that tends to irritate our police friends and they profess not to like 'smart arses' as they so delicately put it."

"Thank you, I must watch what I say."

"Yes, well, let's get back to my question then, you did indeed impersonate a doctor in order to gain access to Mr. Denton?"

"Yes."

"And did you, somehow, encourage him to give you the identities of his two colleagues?"

"Yes."

"Did you do that by injecting some toxic substance into him?"

"No."

"Would you be prepared to tell me how you did so then?"

"Yes."

"Thank you, but before you do that could you explain why you would want to do that in the first place?"

Mason nodded to the folder in front of Trenchard and said, "You may know, I presume, that I was involved in the attack on Richard and Mary Fleming? Involved that is, only in that I intervened in the incident, and although I don't suggest that I actually frightened the attackers away, it was doubtlessly my appearance on the scene that caused them to scarper. I was more concerned with seeing what I could do to help Mrs. Fleming as she had struck her head on the pavement as she fell and was apparently unconscious. I did, though, catch a fleeting glimpse of the three muggers, but all of this, and my description of them, is in the statement that I gave to the police at the time."

"Yes, I know. I have read it."

"Well, a few days after that, I called on Richard to see how they were doing, and he told me that Mary had just died. He was absolutely devastated, as you might imagine, and I felt so terribly sorry for him. That night, I could not get the poor chap out of my mind and, naturally I suppose, it brought back to me the trauma and anguish that I had suffered, and still do, as a result of the attack on my own darling wife. I could not sleep that night, it seemed that the police had not arrested anyone for it, or I'm sure they would have told Richard. Richard told me that he had managed to hit one of them with his walking stick as he fell, and that Sergeant Manners had more or less said that he had been admitted to a hospital. It then occurred to me that it might be helpful if I could somehow get the names of his two mates from whomever it was that Richard had hit. A long shot, of course, because if he hadn't told the police then he certainly wouldn't be inclined to tell me, a complete stranger, and indeed why should he? I wondered how I could get that information from him, so that I could pass it onto the police; I knew that they could not use force or coercion, but perhaps I could fool him in some way? I supposed that the police would say that information gained in that way would be, 'inadmissible', do they call it?"

Trenchard nodded, and Mason continued. "But, if they had some names, I was sure that they would be able to dig around a bit and perhaps find something to link them to it without declaring where the information came from. I didn't know, but it seemed a travesty to me Mr. Trenchard, that vicious thugs like that could get away with that most despicable of all crimes. And it was in the early hours of that morning that the idea came to me. Yes. I know that impersonating a doctor is illegal, but surely the seriousness of that is if it is done for personal gain, or for the procurement of drugs, or to inflict some harm on someone perhaps, but my intention was none of those things."

"Pure altruism, Mr. Mason."

"Yes, absolutely, that is exactly it."

"Thank you, that is very useful, now please tell me how you managed to persuade Mr. Denton to give you those names."

"I assume that my means of effecting entry into Denton's room is now a matter of record?"

"Indeed so."

"OK. When I entered his room, I closed the door and closed the blind on the door's window before I spoke to Denton. I felt his wound, pressed it, actually, and it obviously pained him so I told him that I would inject a strong pain killer to ease his distress. I had a small syringe, without a needle, which I filled with cold water from the jug on his bedside table and injected a quantity of it into the cannula on his arm. I chose cold water so that he would know that something had entered his vein. I then held my hand over his mouth so that he could not call out and told him that what I had injected was not a pain killer but an extremely virulent nerve agent which, unless the antidote was administered within ten minutes, would cause him the most excruciating death."

Trenchard's eyes widened but he did not interrupt.

"He couldn't give me the information that I asked for quickly enough and, when I was satisfied that he wasn't lying, I put an empty syringe onto his cannula to pretend that I was administering the antidote. I told him that it might be uncomfortable for a few minutes, but it was essential that he remained still, and quiet, for at least five minutes, then I left."

Trenchard blew out the breath that he had been unwittingly holding, nodded his head slowly and said, "And this 'antidote' you administered was, in fact, an empty syringe?"

"Yes."

"Tell me, Mr. Mason, have you any medical or nursing training or experience?"

"None whatsoever, in fact I didn't even pass my First Aider's badge when I was in the Scouts."

"So, and this is an observation not a question, you would have been unlikely to have known that injecting a syringe full of air into a vein was likely to induce a heart attack, or a stroke."

"Oh, is that what happened?"

"The pathologist who conducted the Postmortem on Mr. Denton has certified that the cause of death was a massive cardiac arrest, heart attack that is, cause by an embolism, an air bubble, which had been injected into his vein."

"Good Heavens!"

Trenchard suppressed a smile then said, "So why did you bother with the second injection, when you could have just left?"

"Because I had promised him that, if he answered my questions truthfully, I would administer the antidote to the nerve agent. Had I not appeared to have done so he would likely have been screaming the place down before I got out of the door. And, naturally, I wanted to leave the ward without any fuss. So, I pretended to inject the antidote as promised."

"So why not just another shot of water? That would have satisfied him, one would have thought, and could have caused no harm."

"I thought that he would probably have expected it to feel different to the first injection. Had it felt the same he might have thought that it was more 'nerve agent', resulting in even more panic, which, naturally, I wished to avoid."

"Good. Good. So, what we have here, Mr. Mason is, I will submit, an unfortunate, but quite unforeseen, accidental death."

"So, it would seem, Sir, yes."

"They might wonder, of course, why you put your hair dye and contact lenses into Colin Jacques' rubbish bin. They will assume that your intention was to 'frame' him for the attack on Denton and perhaps, who knows, that on Peters."

"Peters? Who is Peters?"

"Oh, I see. Right, well we'll come to him in a moment, but first, let us return to Jacques' wheelie bin, shall we?"

"Denton had given me Jacques' name and address, so I drove past it just to see what sort of place he lived in and, as I did so, I realised that I still had the contact lenses etc with me and I saw that the lazy so-and-so left his bins out at the front of his house, so it seemed a good opportunity to get rid of them. Of course, I didn't expect the police to search the bins, after all I had no way of knowing that they even knew of Jacques, so no, it was not my intention to 'frame' him for anything."

"That's very good. Whether the good Chief Inspector will choose to believe it or not though is another thing all together, although it sounds perfectly reasonable to me.

"Now, before we come on to Mr. Peters, may I ask you if you shop, or have ever shopped, at the Elmington branch of Screwbase?"

"Yes, from time to time."

"And what sort of things do you usually buy there?"

"Well screws, naturally and wall plugs, and a month or so ago I bought myself a new cordless drill. Also, on occasion, I buy stuff there for the Players. My main activity is the sound and lights, but I often help the stage manager with props and stage dressing. He still works for a living, poor soul, so I usually do the shopping for him. My most recent purchase for him was, I believe, some shelf brackets. But why do you ask?"

"So, you could be considered to be a regular customer there, then?"

"I wouldn't say regular, no. Perhaps every couple of months or so, although I do have a loyalty card. In fact, I have one for the Players, too. But what does this have to do with anything?"

Trenchard again ignored the question. "Have you ever bought a packet of cable ties there?"

"Cable ties? I can't imagine what I would need those for."

"So, if a shop assistant, or perhaps the manager, were to say that they sold you a packet of cable ties, what would be your reaction?"

"I would say that they were mistaken. No doubt they probably sell them, and they may well have seen me in the shop from time to time, but I always get a receipt for anything I buy, and especially for the Players and one's name and customer number is printed on the receipt."

"I think that Chief Inspector Parker might suggest that you did buy some, but gave Colin Jacques' name and address as the customer."

"That seems a bit fanciful to me, if I may say so, but why would he think that?"

"Because a packet of Screwbase brand cable ties was found under the front seat of a van belonging to Colin Jacques when his property was searched. At the same time, incidentally, that they found the other items that you had conveniently left in his rubbish bin."

"Well, perhaps, then Mr. Jacques bought them, did that not occur to them? If he had, there is every chance, I would think, that Screwbase would have a record of the sale."

"Yes, that did indeed occur to them, and please don't make the mistake of thinking that the police are stupid, Mr. Mason. They, and in particular DCI Parker, are very astute indeed and are nobody's fools."

"I'm sorry, and I didn't mean to infer that they were. Did they check that, though?"

"Yes, of course they did, and yes, there was a record of such a sale to Mr. Colin Jacques, but they are, none the less, suspicious."

"Are you going to tell me the significance of the cable ties, Mr. Trenchard?"

"Yes, Mr. Mason, I will. Some cable ties, identical to those found in Mr. Jacques' van, were involved in an incident concerning Mr. Peters."

"You mentioned him before, am I supposed to know him?"

"It seems likely that Denton may have given you his name, together with Jacques' when you, er, questioned him that evening."

"No. The other name that Denton gave me was a Freddy Winters of eighty-four Trenton Drive, Kings Dalton. The trouble is that there is no eighty-four Trenton Drive, the numbers there go up only to sixty, so I think that the bugger, I beg your pardon, was lying to me."

"Lying? When he was terrified that he would die the 'most excruciating death' as you put it, if he did?"

"Well, there *is* no number eighty-four Trenton Drive, so what else am I to think? And there is no F Winters in the phone book either, I checked."

"I see. Well, Mr. Mason, it will be important that you stick to that story whilst you are being questioned by Mr. Parker or whomever."

"Story? But you told me not to lie to you, Mr. Trenchard."

"Yes, Mr. Mason and I do not infer that you do."

"Thank you, Sir. So, what about this Mr. Peters then? You

have my curiosity well and truly aroused."

"A Mr. Cecil John Peters, usually known as 'Zack' Peters met an untimely death on Friday the twenty-fifth of this month as a result of being garrotted with some of the afore mentioned cable ties."

"Garrotted? Good God! And you think that I...?"

"I do not think any such thing Mr. Mason, but I fear that DCI Parker might incline to that view. Our task is to convince him that you did not, or preferably, that you could not have."

"But why would he even think that I could possibly want to kill someone that I had never heard of, let alone knew?"

"Possibly because you saw him when you intervened in the attack on the Flemings, and because he had a pony-tail, and that might have stirred memories of the time when your wife was attacked and severely injured, possibly by a thug with a pony-tail. And, I think he might argue, that you are still grieving for the loss of your wife; for the loss of her company if not actually her life, and that some idea of vengeance may therefore have been your motivation."

"Well, that is a strange and convoluted clutching of straws if ever I heard one. Certainly, I grieve for the loss of my wife, and I will never get over that, nor will I ever forgive the scum that struck her, but to think that I would seek revenge on someone just because they have a ponytail? Really? Who does he think I am? The Lone Ranger?"

Trenchard leant forward and put his hand on Mason's arm. "No Mr. Mason. I am sorry that I had to put you through that, but it is likely that the police will adopt this line of enquiry although I now firmly believe that they have absolutely nothing to connect you to 'Zack' Peters. I think though, that there is every chance that DCI Parker will want to charge you with manslaughter in regard to the death of Harry Denton and we really must dissuade him from that if at all possible. Because, you see, manslaughter is a very serious charge indeed. It is what is known as an 'indictable-only' offence and, as such, can be tried only in a Crown Court although a Magistrate, or more probably a District Judge, has the discretion to grant bail if he or she thinks fit. Manslaughter is defined in law as *'where death is the result of behaviour that is grossly negligent'* and carries a starting tariff of twelve years, which would not apply here, or *'where death is caused by an unlawful and dangerous act'* and the starting tariff for that is eighteen years. And it is an unlawful act of manslaughter *'if it is proved that the accused intentionally did an unlawful and dangerous act from which death inadvertently resulted.'* So, we must be prepared to argue that the death was accidental, inadvertent and most certainly *not* with any malicious intent and that you did not *intentionally* perform an unlawful act. Do you follow me?"

Mason nodded. "Indeed, I do."

"Then I would like to suggest that we prepare a statement for you to read out to DCI Parker when he comes to interview you. If we construct it with enough thought and care, it might well anticipate most of his questions and quite possibly satisfy him that you were, if not totally blameless, at least that you had acted without malice. He may, of course, still wish to charge you with impersonating a doctor but, as you have already pointed out to me, you will argue that it was not done for any personal gain or for any of the other reasons that could add gravity to the charge. So do you agree that we should do that?"

"Most certainly, yes."

Simon Trenchard opened his brief case and withdrew a pad of ruled paper which he laid carefully on the table separating him from Arthur Mason, then took a slim, gold pen from his pocket and said, "I suggest that I write the statement along the lines of our discussion, and will read it to you as I go. You may, of course, suggest any addition or amendment at any time. OK?"

"More than OK, Sir, for sure."

"Good, then here we go." He starting to write in a strong cursive hand, pausing occasionally to query or clarify a point with Mason who watched in silence.

After almost twenty minutes he laid his pen down and read the statement to Mason.

"That is absolutely masterful, Sir, if I may say so, and exactly right."

"Thank you. Are you prepared to read this to Mr. Parker, and to sign it as a true account of the events upon which he will wish to question you?"

"I most certainly am."

"Excellent. Then are we ready to meet the good Chief Inspector?"

"Yes Sir, it seems that will be inevitable."

Forty-One

DCI Parker stood up from his desk and stretched, 'Simon is taking his time with Arthur Mason,' he thought, 'and that does not bode well for me, knowing what a clever, or devious, bugger he is'. He switched on the kettle on his filing cabinet and dropped a tea bag into his mug just as his phone rang. He stifled a curse and sat back down at his desk. "DCI Parker."

"Inspector Pritchard here from the drug squad, Sir, I have some news for you concerning your Colin Jacques, which I think you might like, and which I'm sure will amuse Dave Manners."

"Oh, thank you, John, I could do with some good news." He listened intently and a smile spread over his grizzled features. "Oh, that is lovely, John. I think my erstwhile sergeant may well wet his knickers when I tell him that. Thank you."

He opened his door and called, "Dave, when you have a minute, please."

"When I have a minute? Please? This is ominous, it's usually 'Get your arse in here. Now'."

Parker pointed to the chair in front of his desk and leant back in his chair. Suppressing a grin he said, "I have just received some news, sergeant, that impinges on some of the investigations that you have been conducting of late."

"Oh?"

"Inspector Pritchard of the drug squad, whom I believe, you know, has been kind enough to pass on to me some news which is relevant to us, but more for information that action, and he especially asked me to share it with you."

'Well get on with it and stop waffling,' he thought, but said, "So please do that, Guv."

"Following your suggestion, Dave, they examined the computer belonging to one Alistair Jon Fairburn, landlord of the New Moon nightclub. They felt that they had no cause, at that time, to confiscate it, so dear John Pritchard parked one of his jolly crew in Jonny's office to trawl through his list of members and compare those names with the initials in Colin Jacques' notebook. And guess what?"

"By the grin on your mug, Guv, they found a match."

"They did indeed, my boy, and what a match! The initials E M appeared in Jacques' book with the utmost regularity, every two weeks to be exact, and each time for the same amount, two thousand pounds, so obviously E M was a big distributor of his goods."

"E M? No, that means nothing to me."

"Oh, but E M turns out to be Edward, or Teddy, Matthews, a very long-time member of the New Moon indeed."

"No, Guv, as far as I know I didn't come across anyone of that name there."

"Oh, but you did, David, me lad. Edward, Teddy, Matthews. Or perhaps you know him better as 'Estelle'?"

Dave's eyes widened and his mouth dropped open. "Estelle? Oh my God, that is priceless, and of course, as barman was perfectly placed to pass the stuff to his customers. 'And something for the weekend Sir?'"

"Yes, but it gets better. Where do you suppose he concealed his little foil packets?"

Dave laughed. "Up his jacksie, I wouldn't wonder!"

"Not quite. But close! When they searched his home, they

found two of those short frilly skirts that you mentioned, and both had a row of small pockets stitched to the inside of the bottom hem at the front, each of which held a small twist of metal foil containing a dose of heroin identical to the stuff we found under Jacques' bath. And around the hem at the back were slightly larger pockets which Pritchard assumes would hold the folded notes that he received in return."

"Oh, Guvnor, that is just perfect. But is there anything to connect Jon Fairburn to any of this?"

"Inspector Pritchard didn't say, but naturally, their investigations are 'ongoing'."

"Oh, I love you, Guvnor!"

"Here, steady on! We don't want any of that New Moon language in here!"

They both laughed and Manners made his way back to his desk with a spring in his step and a big grin on his face.

Forty-Two

DCI Parker and DC Corbett entered the interview room where Trenchard and Mason were already seated. They nodded acknowledgement to Trenchard and took their seats opposite. Corbett removed the wrappers from two new tape cassettes and inserted them into the recorder, then ran through the introductory routine. He and Parker introduced themselves and indicated for Mason and Trenchard to do the same.

The formalities over, Parker said, "Mr. Mason, I would remind you that you are under arrest on suspicion of murder, and you are still under caution, do you understand that?"

"Yes."

Trenchard raised a hand to attract Parker's attention and when the DCI raised his eyebrows questioningly Simon said, "Detective Chief Inspector, my client has a prepared statement that he wishes to read to you. Would that be acceptable?"

Parker looked from Mason to Trenchard and back. "Yes, go ahead."

"Thank you, Chief Inspector. Mr. Mason?"

Mason cleared his throat and took a sip of water from the glass at his elbow and said, "I am Arthur Mason, and I wish to offer the following statement." He then read out the paper which Simon Trenchard had prepared and which he had agreed was an acceptable version of the events that had led to his arrest. Both Parker and Corbett listened intently, Parker making an occasional note on a pad in front of him. Once or twice Corbett made as if to interrupt, but Parker raised a hand to silence him. When he had finished, he took a longer drink from the glass and sat back, looking at Parker expectantly.

"Thank you for that, Mr. Mason. So, you admit that you impersonated a doctor?"

"Yes, I have said so."

"And, as a result of this impersonation, you forced your way into Harry Denton's room in Bolton Ward in Elmington General Hospital?"

"Certainly not. There was no force involved whatsoever, in fact your Constable opened the door for me."

"Maybe so, but you entered his room under false pretences and then assaulted him."

"Not at all, Sir. I did not assault him."

"Not physically perhaps, but mentally then?"

"No. I may have frightened him a little but there was certainly no assault."

"You assaulted him by injecting a substance into his vein."

"Water, Chief Inspector, water. I injected a small amount of water, and with his consent I must say."

"But he didn't know it was simply water, did he?"

"Obviously not."

"He thought that it was an extremely toxic substance that, if the antidote was not administered within a certain time, would kill him."

"My client has already explained all that, Chief Inspector, and quite cogently, I would suggest."

"And I wonder just where the cogency of that statement originated, Mr. Trenchard?"

"I object to the implication in that comment, Chief Inspector. I can assure you that my client is quite capable of compiling a statement of the facts of the matter, and any suggestion that I have put words into his mouth is totally unfounded and insulting in the extreme."

"All right, Mr. Trenchard, I was not implying any impropriety here."

"Then will you accept that his statement is just that? A statement of facts?"

"No. You see, I do not believe you Mr. Mason. I believe that, having effected your entry into Mr. Denton's room by means of subterfuge, as you've admitted, you extracted from him the information that you wanted and then deliberately injected a volume of air into his vein, knowing that it was likely to result in a heart attack or a stroke and, subsequently, his death."

"My client has already said, Chief Inspector, that he did not *intentionally* inject air into Mr. Denton. What he did was to *pretend* to inject something so that Denton would think he was administering the fictitious antidote. Indeed, he has explained that he did not even screw the syringe into the cannula, he merely held it there and, in fact, did not expect anything to go into the vein, but even it if did, he had no reason whatever to believe that mere air could possibly have the results that it apparently did."

"Possibly. But I am not convinced, Mr. Mason, that you did not put those items of disguise, shall we say, into Mr. Jacques' wheelie bin without the intention of implicating him in the death of Harry Denton."

"Those items were put there, Chief Inspector, exactly for the reason that I have explained in my statement. And I will reiterate that I had no reason to think that his bin would be searched, or even that you knew of him, or indeed that those bins would not have been emptied within a few days. And nor, critically, could I have expected Mr. Denton to die, so why would the police have any interest in Mr. Jacques?"

"All right, let's leave that for the moment. Now, what about those cable ties?"

"As I have already explained, before Mr. Trenchard spoke to me earlier this afternoon, I knew nothing whatsoever about any cable ties, and if this somehow relates to the death of Mr. Peters, let me assure you, again, Chief Inspector, that I had never heard the name before Mr. Trenchard mentioned it during our earlier conversation."

"Indeed, Chief Inspector, I believe that you have no evidence whatsoever to cause you to think that my client knew Mr. Peters, far less that he was involved in any way with his death, and I would be obliged if you would refrain from pestering him with irrelevant questions and insinuations which, one can only assume, have the intention of causing him unwarranted distress."

"But you shop regularly at Screwbase, where the cable ties were purchased, do you not?"

"No, not regularly. Occasionally yes, but I have never bought cable ties there, even for the use of the Elmington Players. As I understand it, though, there is evidence that Mr. Jacques bought some, isn't there?"

"This interview might go more easily, Mr. Mason, if we revert to the old-fashioned method whereby we ask the questions and you answer them."

"If they are relevant, Chief Inspector, of course."

"So, you positively deny putting those cable ties into Mr. Jacques' van?"

"I have already..." He sighed. "Yes, Chief Inspector, I positively deny putting those cable ties into Mr. Jacques' van."

"Then how do suppose they got there?" interposed Corbett.

"I am sorry, Constable, but I did not think that I was here to offer any suppositions, or theories, on matters of which I cannot possibly have any knowledge. But, if it helps, I dare say that it might just be possible that Mr. Jacques did indeed buy them for whatever purpose, as your evidence would suggest or, if they were used on the unfortunate Mr. Peters, as you seem to infer, then possibly by whomever killed him."

"You don't seem particularly upset or surprised to hear of the death of Mr. Peters do you, Mr. Mason?" said Corbett, stinging slightly at the perceived insult.

"Well, Constable, at the risk of sounding trite, I could say that any death, particularly a violent one, is to be regretted but, as I had never met him, nor even heard of him, then surely it should not be a surprise that I am not unduly upset. The only upsetting thing to me is that I should be accused of his death, and that is deeply upsetting, I assure you."

"Will that be all, Chief Inspector? I think my client has more than adequately answered all your allegations."

"Possibly, Mr. Trenchard, but I am still minded to charge him with impersonating a doctor with intent to cause distress to a suspect in our custody. I may prepare a case for the CPS to consider."

"Oh, come now, Chief Inspector, let us be realistic for just a moment, please. I am unaware of any such charge as 'intent to cause distress' and, although Mr. Denton may have been a suspect, he was definitely *not* in your custody. He was an NHS patient in an NHS Hospital. He had not been arrested, had he?"

"No, but-"

"No 'buts', Chief Inspector, please. Pass whatever you have to the Crown Prosecution Service if you wish but I would be very surprised if they would agree that there is a reasonable chance of a successful prosecution along the lines that you suggest."

"Well, I might still charge him with 'impersonating a doctor' which, you may remember, he has already admitted."

"Of course, you might, but that would rather smack of spite don't you think? Of sour grapes? A poor loser perhaps? And really, Chief Inspector, I thought better of you than that."

Parker gathered up his papers, nudged Corbett and said, "This interview is terminated at five-fourty-seven p.m." Then, after Corbett had removed the cassettes from the recorder, addressed Mason. "You will now be returned to your cell, Mr. Mason, in custody, to await my decision as to what further action would be appropriate."

***

Back in Parker's office, Simon took the seat indicated and said, "So you intend to charge him, then?"

"Of course. I have no choice really, he has already admitted the impersonation, after all. And we really can't have people taking the law into their own hands, however justified or altruistic they may think they are."

"Yes. Well, in that case I think I will represent him in court, pro bono, obviously."

"But he will plead guilty, so is that necessary?"

"Perhaps not, but even so. I would not like to see him savaged by that Rottweiler of yours, without at least some moral support, he might even get him to admit shooting J F Kennedy!"

"Rottweiler? You mean young Corbett? Oh, don't think too badly of him. He's young and he will learn. But in fairness to him, Simon, it was his investigation that led us to Mason, you know."

"Really? I thought that was down to PC Carter, or did I misread your notes?"

"Now who's splitting hairs?"

"OK, point taken, but I will offer Mr. Mason my support in court, anyway. To be honest, Reg, I have rather taken to the old chap, indeed his remark that he thought legal representation would not be necessary might have been nearer the mark than we thought."

"Well, he's nobody's fool, I'll give you that, but what the outcome of that interview might have been without your advice, Simon, is anybody's guess."

Forty-Three

Sergeant Manners unlocked DCI Parker's office and surveyed the piles of paperwork on his desk in dismay. He had just received a phone call from his boss to say that he had tested positive for COVID and was therefore now in self-isolation, but would, naturally, be at the end of a phone line should his sergeant need him, meanwhile would David be kind enough to hold the fort for him whilst he 'worked at home'? He sat in Parker's chair and looked at the pile of messages in his in-tray and, as he switched on the computer, saw that there were a couple of dozen emails awaiting his attention. 'Oh, Lord,' he thought, 'so this is what the old man gets up to, when we all thought he was playing Solitaire?' As he clicked on the first email the phone rang. "DCI Parker's office, Sergeant Manners speaking."

"Front Desk here, Dave, I have a gentleman here who wishes to have a word with you."

"OK, put him on then."

"No, he wants to see you Dave, he says that he has something that he wants to show you."

"Who is he?"

"A Mr. Tony Fleming."

"Oh, well, send him up straight away, please, I can't come down just now, but get someone to bring him up to Mr. Parker's office if you would."

"Of course, Dave, will do."

After a few minutes, there was a knock on the door and Tony

Fleming was ushered in.

Manners got to his feet and shook hands. "Good to see you, Tony, please take a seat, and don't be alarmed at the office here, I am not suffering with delusions of grandeur, but my boss has just tested positive to this dreadful pestilence and has left me to keep his seat warm."

"Thank you, Sergeant."

"No, it's Dave, please."

"OK, then Dave, firstly I want to thank you, and Mr. Lee, for your kindness to my Dad, it meant a lot to him and Sally and I really appreciate it."

Manners frowned. "Meant?"

"Yes. I'm afraid Dad died two nights ago."

"Oh no, Tony, I am so sorry. But, how?"

"He took his own life, Dave. An overdose, assisted, I'm sad to say, by the bottle of his favourite single malt that Sally had given him after Mum's funeral. Sally and I were staying with him for a while after the funeral and I'm so glad that we were. Two days ago, I took a cup of coffee up for him in the morning and saw this note stuck on his bedroom door. It was marked, 'Tony, please read this before you come in'. I knew of course as soon as I saw it. I sat on the bed with Sally, and it must have been an hour before I could bring myself to open it. And I would like you to read it."

"But how, Tony? Overdoses these days are not as simple as the popular press would have us believe. Medication is so carefully monitored and regulated that-"

"Yes, I know, Dave, but I believe I know exactly what he did. Years ago he suffered with arthritis in his knees and eventually had the right one replaced. But before that his GP had prescribed distalgesic tablets for his pain and Dad swore by them.

They were replaced by, or renamed, perhaps, co-proximal but, in about 2007 I think it was, they were withdrawn. Dad's GP told me that they were no longer allowed to prescribe them as they were thought to be responsible for a large number of deaths, both intentional and accidental and their presence was difficult to detect, even in a postmortem. Dad's GP, bless his heart, supplied Dad with them for as long as he could though, and I believe that he had some stashed away somewhere for when his pain became unbearable. Of course, if Mum had ever found them, she would have turfed them out; she was obsessed by 'use by' dates and any that Dad had must surely have been well past it, but still effective, I'm sure. The old distalgesic tablets had 'DG' impressed on them and Dad always said that stood for 'Dei Gratia', his 'Thank God tablets', he called them. The only things that eased his pain. In truth, they were not nearly so effective as many of the other analgesics that were available at the time."

Tony drew in a deep breath and exhaled it in a long sigh. "Well, they've eased all his pain now."

He pushed the envelope across the table to Dave. "Please."

Dave took the envelope with a shaking hand and withdrew a single sheet of paper, handwritten. He glanced at Tony who nodded to him.

Dear Tony and Sally,

I am so sorry to do this to you, but I cannot live like this – without my darling Mary. I have tried, these last few days, to come to terms with this terrible grief but I know that I never can. We had loved each other so much for so long and I consider myself to have been the luckiest of men.

I suspect, Tony, that you will know that this was the final help from my Thank God tablets, even though the writing on the little tub has faded beyond recognition, so I hope that may avoid the necessity of a postmortem, for your sakes.

I sincerely hope that you can understand and find it in your hearts to forgive me. I believe that two of the evil creatures that did this have met their own deaths and that the third is facing the possibility of a lifetime in prison. Justice, perhaps, in a way, but no consolation, Tony. Oh, no, there is no consolation.

Just one favour I would ask of you please, if, or when, anybody asks, just tell them that I died of a broken heart.

With all my love,
Dad

Manners handed the letter back to Tony Fleming.

A tear rolled unashamedly down his cheek as he whispered a barely audible, "Thank you."